SECRETS OF A RUNAWAY BRIDE

SECRETS OF MUSTANG ISLAND

SYLVIA MCDANIEL

❀ Created with Vellum

Running Away Brought Her What She Wanted

Crystal Young isn't marrying for love, but it will give her what her heart desires until her fiancé reveals his true treacherous self. Running, she takes their honeymoon cruise alone. While on the cruise, a crazy encounter with the man next door pushes her over the edge. Giving up on men, she returns home determined to have a baby on her own.

Attorney Tyler Nelson wonders why his best friend and client billionaire has been acting strange. When he learns of his client's latest business deal, he advises against it. And then when Tyler learns the deal is with the crazy woman from the cruise ship, he's incredulous. The woman is bonkers and not fit to be a mother.

Crystal will do whatever it takes to have a baby. Only the revelation of devastating secrets could change Tyler's mind. Secrets that will transform everything including Crystal's dreams.

CHAPTER 1

*A*t thirty-eight years of age, her time was running out to achieve the dream she so desperately wanted. Crystal Young yearned for a family she no longer had.

And yet sitting alone in the bridal waiting room, her anxiety was through the roof.

Was she making the right decision?

Yes, Aaron had agreed she could get pregnant immediately, so there was that point in his favor, but did she really love him? Love him enough to spend the rest of her life with him? Wake up beside him each morning?

Why did everything feel so off? Even her friends had told her this was not a good idea. Marriage was hard, and yet she wanted a normal family.

One that spent holidays together. One to go through life's misadventures, its fun moments, and even its worst times. One where your father would walk you down the aisle, and your mother would help the first month after the grandchild was born.

A family to replace everything she'd lost and more.

With a sigh, she glanced at the clock. Their cruise ship would be leaving in two hours. Time to make a decision.

A decision that seemed to bear down on her like the weight of the planet. A decision that had serious consequences. To her, marriage was forever.

If this marriage was meant to be, shouldn't she be happy? Wouldn't she have gotten past the doubts? The anxiety?

Why did this feel so wrong?

A knock at the door had her jumping.

Standing, she scuttled to the door in the short silk dress she'd chosen. The dress was more for an after-five occasion, and yet she hadn't wanted the long-flowing gown. Nothing about this wedding was the same as she'd dreamed of years ago.

Opening the door, Spencer Duncan, Aaron's best friend stood in front of her. His eyes were dark and ominous and a serious expression graced his handsome face.

Aaron was backing out…

"May I come in?" Spencer asked.

"Of course," she said. "Is something wrong? Has Aaron changed his mind?"

Why did relief surge through her at the thought? Another signal that this wedding was all wrong.

"No," Spencer said, "but there's something you need to know before you agree to marry him. I've not slept the last two nights trying to decide whether to do what was right or keep my mouth shut. I've got to tell you the truth."

This sounded strange. What did she need to know?

Nervous, she licked her lips as an unwelcome tingle centered in the pit of her stomach. What kind of secrets was her fiancé hiding?

"Aaron has not been honest with you. He's in financial trouble, so his mother has basically bought him. She wants grandchildren, an heir. By marrying you, he can give her that and she'll pay off his debts."

That seemed odd. When they talked, he acted like he had plenty of money. And they couldn't wait to have children together. She wanted at least three and had to get started now before the clock ran out. It was one of the reasons she'd said yes to his proposal. And now she was doubting herself.

"I didn't know about his financial troubles, but we both want children," she said, alarm bells ringing as she suddenly thought about how Spencer was always around Aaron.

"Being with me, we could never have children unless we adopted," Spencer said. "His mother wants the family line to continue. She thinks you can *cure* him."

Like a smack to the forehead, she suddenly realized what was going on. How could she have been so blind?

"Aaron is your lover," she said breathlessly.

Spencer's shoulders relaxed and his posture completely changed. His expression softened and he seemed to turn into a different person, like the man she'd been introduced to not too long ago wasn't the real Spencer.

"Yes, darling, he is," he said, using a word he'd never used around her. "And he has no intention of giving me up," he said. "That's not fair to you or to me."

Stunned, she sank like a rock into the nearest chair. Her dress slid up her thighs, but she didn't even try to pull it down. Nobody in this room was interested.

"All this time, I've wondered why he seemed aloof when it came to sex between us, and now I know why. He didn't want me; he wanted you," she said, hurt causing her chest to ache.

Aaron wanted another man, not her.

Spencer stood there, shaking his head. "Darling, I'm sorry to be the one to tell you, but this wedding is a huge mistake. And once you have the baby, the grandmother plans on fighting for custody. You will come out of this with nothing."

Now she understood all the feelings of doubt. The feelings of anxiety. The universe had been trying to warn her that she was making a colossal blunder, but she kept pushing forward. Pushing to get what she wanted, whether it was the right thing or not. Damn her determination.

When her chin fell to her chest, the first tear trickled down her cheek.

It wasn't like she was madly in love with Aaron. He was just a means to get what she wanted.

"I wish you had told me sooner," she said.

He hung his head for a moment. "I've been fighting with myself for the last month, and this week, it became unbearable. This morning, I knew I had to tell you."

Looking up at him, she saw tears in the corners of his eyes.

"Thank you for letting me know."

"If he learns I spoke to you, I'll lose him," Spencer said. "And his witch of a mother, she will cut him off for not getting what she wants."

There would be no wedding. There would be no baby in nine months. There would be no family. Her friends were gathered, waiting in the parlor for her to walk down the aisle, and now she couldn't face anyone.

Aaron was gay.

She'd almost married a gay man. It wasn't that she faulted him for being gay, just for lying to her and hiding the fact his mother would take any child they produced.

Crystal fought the overwhelming urge to curl up in a ball and cry her heart out, but there was no time.

The cruise. The honeymoon suite awaited them.

She needed time to think, to mend, and it was too late to cancel the trip she'd promised herself she would get pregnant on. She was getting on that boat. The limo sat out front of the mansion they were being married in.

Looking up, she gazed at Spencer. How had she missed all the telltale signs that he was gay? Aaron was gay. If he'd told her the truth, she would have wished him the best and walked away.

Now she felt humiliated that she'd refused to see the evidence when it was right in front of her face. She was a fool for letting herself believe she'd found a man who would love her and give her the family she longed for.

"Where's the back door?"

"Follow me," he said. "That's the way I came in."

She grabbed the carry-on bag she'd packed for tonight that held her white sexy nightie. Damn him.

Tears bubbled up, but she couldn't let go. Not yet. There would be plenty of time for crying once she got away. Right now, she had to escape. She had to part ways with this disastrous wedding. No wonder Aaron's mother had always looked at her like thinking *you poor fool*. Now she knew. Now she understood.

Looking around the room, she made sure she had everything. One more screw-up on her part. One more wrong choice.

It was time for her to forget her dreams. Time for her to face reality. She was meant to be alone.

"Let's go," she said.

When he opened the door, she heard the music. They were all waiting for her to walk down the grand stairs and say her vows. Well, they would be waiting until hell froze over.

Spencer peeked out of the bride's chamber, and together, the two of them tiptoed down the hall to the servants' stairs in the historic home in Galveston, Texas – a place she'd found on the internet not far from the cruise's docking station.

A ship she would be taking alone.

They hurried down the stairs. The caterers were busy setting up the food for the reception. She glanced at them. "Donate all of it to a homeless shelter."

"What?" the director said, her eyes growing large.

"Give the food to a homeless shelter. There will be no wedding today. There will be no reception. I'm leaving."

With that, she walked out of the kitchen and through the back door. After hurrying around to the front, she turned to Spencer when they reached the limo.

"Thank you for telling me. Tell Aaron I said…" What did she want to say to him? Only one thing came to mind and she didn't want to use that word. "Tell him I said don't ever contact me again. I wish him the best of luck. And Spencer you deserve better."

The man grinned. "If only I didn't love him."

"If he loved you, he would not have agreed to marry me," she said. "I hope you find someone who deserves you."

"You too," he said and hugged her.

She slipped the ring off her finger and handed it to Spencer. "Give it back to him, wear it, do whatever you want with that rock."

Gazing down at the jewelry in his hand, he shook his head, laughing. "It should have been mine."

"Yes, it should've been."

She climbed into the limo, closed the door, and rolled down the window to wave good-bye.

The door of the house opened and Aaron ran down the stairs, waving his arms wildly. "Stop. Where are you going? Spencer, you didn't tell her, did you?"

Shaking her head, tears filled her eyes. "Go, driver, now."

"Yes, ma'am," he said.

She pulled her mother's long white-lace wedding veil from her head as she sank against the leather seats. The car sped down the drive and pulled onto the street.

"Take me to the cruise ship," she told the driver. "At least one of us is going on our honeymoon."

CHAPTER 2

*T*yler Nelson often had trouble sleeping and tonight was no exception. It had been his sister's idea to take their mother on a cruise for her eightieth birthday. A chance for them to all be together. Thank goodness they had rented a suite with two bedrooms and a large balcony that overlooked the ocean.

Sitting outside on the deck in the darkness, he was shocked to see that the divider between their suite and the suite next door had fallen. He'd have to mention that to the steward in the morning. No need to bother their neighbors.

Especially with his nocturnal wanderings.

But sitting out on the balcony in the darkness was calming as he listened to the boat slide through the ocean water and gazed up at the millions of stars that guided them toward the Bahamas.

Seven days they would all be together. Seven days of partying on a boat. Sure he loved his sister and his mother, but that was a long time to listen to two women yammer about anything and everything, who often argued over the most ridiculous things.

Two women who had hated each other when they were growing up and made their family life hell.

Hopefully this week, he would have the time to relax, recover, and prepare for the next six months. His biggest client and closest friend had been acting strange, and when he got back, he wanted to sit down and talk to him about what was going on in his life.

The man had suddenly withdrawn into himself and no matter how Tyler acted like a goofball around him, he wasn't responding like before. Something was wrong, but he wasn't saying what was eating at him. Even his color was off.

After his last girlfriend broke up with him, David had said he was done with women. But not Tyler. In fact, if his mother and sister weren't with him, he would be trying to pick up someone. Still might try, but those two would scrutinize his every move, and there would be no bringing a woman back to the cabin.

Besides, women were often more trouble than they were worth. Just once, he'd like to meet a woman who didn't care about how much money he made. They didn't need to know he was worth billions and that he only worked because he loved what he did for a living.

Lawyers were not all rich, but he came from a long line of lawyers, clear back to the Constitution. Or at least that's what his father had told him when he was a young boy.

What his father had not told him about was the insomnia that plagued the men in the family. The women could fall asleep anywhere, but he fought to sleep every night.

And sleeping pills were a nuisance he didn't need. Once they put him to sleep, he didn't want to wake up.

But after being awake for three days, he would often give up and take them. Only problem, he had left them at home. So tonight he would probably sit here and watch the sun come up.

Next door, the sliding glass door opened and a woman walked out carrying something white and lacy in her hands. Her white dress shimmered in the moonlight.

She wadded up whatever she had in her hands and threw it overboard.

That was breaking the rules. Lawyers did not like to see other people breaking the rules.

"You can be fined for throwing things over the deck," he said.

"So fine me, I don't care," she said. "Call the cruise cops and turn me in. Kick me overboard if you must, but that shit had to go."

Oh, great. She was a crazy one.

He heard material rip. What the hell was she doing now?

In the moonlight, he saw her dress being torn from her body. And when the zipper got to the bodice, he could see she was stuck.

"Damn," she cursed, tugging at the dress.

For a moment, she stopped, her breathing labored, and again, she tried to tear the material off her body, but the bodice wouldn't budge.

"Would you do me a favor," she asked. "I know this must seem strange, but would you unhook the back of my dress?"

Oh no, he wasn't going to get caught up in some domestic

violence when her husband came charging out wanting to know what he was doing.

"No, I'm not going to have your husband beat the crap out of me for touching you."

"No husband," she said. "Just me and this damn wedding gown that I can't get off."

Oh, that was interesting. She was stuck in her *wedding* gown? The honeymoon suite was next door, but she was alone. He'd love to hear this tale.

"Why are you alone?" he asked.

"Same question for you," she said. "It's really none of your business. But I ran away from the wedding." She started laughing hysterically. "I guess you could call me a runaway bride."

Damn, that was harsh. Some poor guy was sitting back at home wondering what happened.

"And now I can't get this damn gown off." She lifted a champagne bottle to her lips and took a swig.

The woman was batshit crazy, but he couldn't imagine being trapped in a dress that was a reminder of everything bad that happened. Or had the groom realized she was nuts and called off the wedding?

"Come here," he said. "But don't throw it overboard."

She walked over to the railing that separated the two balconies.

"Lift your hair up," he said, thinking she had beautiful soft blonde tresses that he wanted to run his fingers through. And she smelled like soft summer rain. Refreshing.

"A complete stranger unhooking this damn dress," she said. "Tonight, he was supposed to help me undress. We were supposed to be celebrating with champagne and chocolates and having the best night of sex we'd ever experienced. Instead, I'm in this wasted wedding dress and drinking champagne alone. Would you like some? I'm planning on getting thoroughly drunk."

It appeared she already was there.

He reached the last hook and unfastened it. The dress slid to the balcony floor, leaving her in a strapless bra, and a silky white thong.

Bending over she picked up the dress, her white smooth buttocks glistening in the moonlight. Damn!

Before he could stop her, she threw the wedding gown overboard.

"Didn't I ask you not to throw anything else overboard?" he said, staring at her beautiful figure in the moonlight. Damn, some man was a fool to let that get away from him. But then again, she was acting like an out-of-control teenager.

"You did, but I did what I had to do. That dress brought me bad luck and I don't need any more of that. Maybe I should have given it to you and then you could have had the bad luck," she said gazing over the side.

For a moment, he was afraid she might try to jump, but yet she didn't act suicidal.

She picked up the champagne bottle and sank down into one of the reclining chairs. "This is my party and I can cry if I want to. You were not supposed to be on the balcony at this time of night. What are you doing out here?"

"I couldn't sleep. Insomnia is my closest friend."

She gave a little sigh. "Once I got to my suite, I fell asleep on the bed. I just woke up and had to get that dreaded dress off."

Did the woman realize she was sitting out here talking to a stranger in her bra and underwear? It was quite the sight. A very enjoyable view, but he thought she must not realize what she was doing because of the champagne.

"Do you know why I called off the wedding?"

She had called off the wedding, not the poor bastard she was to marry.

"No," he said, wondering how he could know. He didn't even know her name.

She laughed. "He's gay. His partner came to me today and told me he was gay. I didn't realize it, but now looking back, how could I have missed the fact that he preferred men?"

She started to cry, which made him uncomfortable. Should he comfort her? But then again, that would mean going to her balcony. Not a wise idea.

"Nothing against gay people. I love them. I've often thought I would be better off being gay than trying to find a man who loves me. I'm now three and zero. Three engagements, no wedding. I'm a three-time wedding loser."

In the darkness, he rolled his eyes. "I've never even come close. So at least you have three misses."

There was silence before she lifted the bottle to her lips. "One told me I wanted too much from him. All I expected was for him to have a job. Is that asking too much? One fell in love with his secretary. They're now happily married with two children and another on the way. And then there is Aaron. How do I get over the man who I believed loved me when, actually, he loved another man?"

She gave a drunken laugh.

"Why are you on this cruise? Why aren't you married with two point five kids?" she asked, turning to look at him.

Oh no, he wanted no part of crazy and she obviously was a lunatic.

"We're celebrating my mom's eightieth birthday. And I've never found a woman who I wanted to marry. I'm an all-in-or-nothing kind of guy. Plus, she'd have to put up with me and my insomnia."

There was a moment of silence before she took another swig.

"That's wonderful," she said. "You're lucky."

Lucky because he was here or because his mother was eighty? Or lucky because he'd not found anyone who'd put up with him?

"Why didn't I realize he was gay?" she mumbled more to herself than to him. "My friends kept telling me if I didn't love him, not to marry him. But I gave up on love a long time ago. Probably right after the second engagement failed."

He didn't know how to answer her. Love had not crossed his doorstep since high school when he fell in love with Cindy McDougal.

"I can't answer that question for you. I haven't loved anyone since I was a teen. She went away to college and I never heard from her again."

"You should look her up," the half-naked woman said.

Did she realize that even in the darkness, he could see her long legs, her full hips, narrow waist, and breasts that he could almost feel in his hands? All he had to do was close his eyes and imagine the touch of her skin against his.

"No, I want to keep my image of her in my mind. My teenage boy fantasies were filled with her. She's probably a mom now, driving a minivan, and attending a food club to lose weight. I'd rather remember her the way she was."

She gave a snort. "I don't have anyone I want to remember like that. You're lucky."

Was he, sitting outside on a balcony unable to sleep and spilling his guts to a half-nude woman who would soon pass out from alcohol?

Suddenly she stood and swayed on the deck. For a moment, he wondered if he would have to climb over the rail and tuck her into bed.

Oh no, that was not going to happen.

"Well, you were my knight in shining armor tonight. You saved me from a dress that had its ugly claws in me and wouldn't let go. Now, I fear I've had too much to drink and will sleep with one foot on the floor and hope that I don't pray to the porcelain god tonight."

He gave a little laugh. That was probably in her future, but he wouldn't tell her.

She went to bow to him but almost fell over. "Goodnight, kind sir. May sleep overcome you. And may Aaron Lewis's balls shrink to the size of peanuts, or even better, be crushed."

That was cruel. But he guessed when you learned that kind of truth on your wedding day, it would devastate you.

"Again, thank you for rescuing me from the dress. Sweet dreams, sir."

She opened the sliding glass doors and walked inside, her bare ass cheeks like a beacon in the pale moonlight. A beacon he was tempted to get up and follow but knew better.

With a sigh, he leaned back and thought about running his hands all over her body. Maybe she would agree to a one-night stand to cleanse her palate of her bad experience with Aaron. Or maybe he should stay away from her because somewhere she had at least one screw loose if not many more.

Never had he experienced a woman sitting on her balcony almost naked. Though the sight had been quite lovely and made his evening rather interesting.

CHAPTER 3

*A*ll week, Crystal stayed locked up in her cabin or sat out on the balcony. Whoever the man was she met, she hadn't seen him since that night when he'd helped her get out of her wedding dress.

That was supposed to have been Aaron's job, but he wasn't here. Thank God.

She'd read several books. Watched a couple of movies, but more than anything, she'd made a list of life decisions. She wanted a family and while she really longed for a man, someone to be the baby's father, she obviously wasn't going to get that. And her biological clock would soon explode, so the time was now.

No more searching for a man. No more looking for love. This week she'd made the decision.

All she needed was a turkey baster with some man's sperm.

There were catalogs with men she could choose from. All she needed to do was find the right candidate, and hopefully soon, she'd be pregnant.

The seven-day cruise had helped heal her wounded spirit and she liked the notebook she'd filled with ideas for how she wanted her life. Now all she had to do was make the right choices.

It was late. Tonight was the last night and she wanted to enjoy the balcony one last time before she had to disembark in the morning.

In her robe, she opened the door and stepped onto the deck. With a sigh, she sank down into the chair and stared at the stars. They looked so close, like you could reach out and touch them.

"Good evening," a voice called. "It's been almost seven days since I've seen you."

"Didn't leave the cabin much," she said. "Wasn't in the mood. How about you? Did you have a nice cruise?"

There was a long silence before he finally answered. "I had a great time. My mother and sister got into a row and haven't spoken for the last two days, but that's women for you. You ladies fight over the stupidest things."

Not necessarily, she thought.

"We fight for what we believe in," she said. "It's you men. You don't understand us and our need to protect the home. We will come after anyone who tries to take what's ours."

He chuckled. "Even a souvenir?"

Well, that was ridiculous, but each woman set her own limits.

"Maybe," she said. "You don't take what's ours."

Except for other men. But then Aaron had never really been hers to take away from. He'd been Spencer's. With a sigh, she pushed the thoughts of him from her head. He was not worth her time.

"But I can't tell you the number of cases I've had where the woman wanted her share of the property and his as well. You don't play very well."

He must be a lawyer. That would explain the fancy suite they were all in.

"Who said we had to play well? Sometimes playing fair just gets you last place. As women, we're acutely aware of the power men have in this world. You guys run just about everything, so we have to pick and choose our battles. And when a marriage ends badly, women can be vicious."

Even when engagements end badly. When she got home, she was going to have her attorney draw up a letter to Aaron asking for half the cost of their disastrous day.

"What battles have you fought?" he asked.

She wasn't going to divulge that information to him. He was a stranger. Someone she would never see again. But then again, wasn't that the perfect person to reveal secrets to?

"Let's just say I'm done with men. I'm going home. I'm going to live my life my way and do things I want to do. And the first order of business is to get pregnant."

That should shock him.

"What? You want nothing to do with men and yet you're going to go out and get pregnant. That's not very logical."

He could think all he wanted to about her plan. But she'd made a very detailed strategy on what to do and the first thing was to make an appointment with her gynecologist just as soon as she got home.

Then she would look through the catalog and decide on what man's sperm she wanted and begin the process of creating her own family. It was past time.

"A child needs a mother and a father," he said. "Believe me, I know."

For a second, she was tempted to ask him how he knew, but she didn't want anyone to change her mind. She'd made her decision. Now it would be time to implement it.

"No, I've tried it the old-fashioned way. I've given up on the idea of love. I've given up on the idea of a traditional family and I'm going to do things my way."

He laughed. "And you're prepared to do the late-night feeding and changes by yourself. To take care of the child when it gets sick and attend teacher conferences alone. To be the only mother at baseball practice? To explain to your son or daughter sex and why it's important not to sleep with everyone? And so much more."

She gave a little laugh. Did the man not understand anything? Maybe there was a reason he was still single.

"Why do you think I'm doing this? I want to be a mother. I want a family. I want to be there by their side as they grow and begin their life," she said, recalling the memory of her mother and father taking her to college. "I want to be the one to drop them off at school. I want to wipe away their tears and help them get a great start in life."

Pain gripped her chest as she remembered saying good-bye to her parents and little sister. And then they were gone.

"But a kid needs both parents," he said. "It's a balance and when there's only one parent, it's off balance."

"Tell that to all the single mothers out there who take care of the family every day."

He sighed. "My mother was a single mother."

"Well, I'm going to do my best to raise balanced, normal

children. With one parent who really loves them. I'm going to be that person."

"You're just thinking of yourself," he said.

Yes, maybe she was, but she had lost everything. And no matter how hard she tried to replace the missing love, she'd been unable to replicate it.

"Maybe there's a reason that you're still single," she said, knowing it was a smartass comment. "Yes, I'm giving up on men. I've tried for almost twenty years and I haven't found one worth having."

"And maybe the reason you're still single is because all you're focused on is getting pregnant," he said.

It was a retaliatory statement that had her chest tightening with pain. And yet, maybe it was true.

The sound of the waves crashing against the boat calmed her.

"You're right. I am focused on creating a family. I'm running out of time and I've given up on finding the 'love' of my life. So now I'm moving on to plan B. A family without a man."

In the darkness, she could see him shaking his head.

"You're a stranger," he said. "Why I'm trying to help you see the truth, I don't know. My father died when I was seven and my sister was four. Shot in the line of duty as he went into a courtroom to convict a man wanted for murder. The idiot thought if he got rid of the prosecutor, the trial would end. Now he's in prison for the rest of his life. So yes, I know exactly the kind of family you're going to try to create. One where the mother becomes the head of the household."

Taking a deep breath, she sighed. She would not talk about

her family situation. It was just too painful. "I'm sorry to hear about your father. I'm thirty-eight years old and I want a child. In fact, I want several children. Yes, I'm going to be just fine as a single mother. It will be better than being married to a man who has his own lover or is involved with his secretary."

"Did you ever think that you were picking the wrong type of men?"

Stunned, she glanced into the darkness at the man. Why was she having such a personal conversation with a stranger?

"Yes, I have," she said. "I've even sought out counseling and look where that led me. To a man who lied to me. Maybe it's me. Maybe I'm unlovable. Maybe I choose the wrong type of men, but I'm over it. This last one did me in. So I'm going forward with having a baby on my own."

Was it because it was dark and he'd seen her at her worst that she could so easily speak to this man, whoever he was? For all she knew, he was divorced, a psychopath, whatever. All she knew about him was that he was a lawyer. A lawyer, who was on a cruise with his mother and sister, who were fighting. And he didn't like fighting.

Yet, he seemed to have picked one with her.

"Look, it's your life. I have no say in this, but I just wanted you to know how a boy who grew up without his father felt. His absence was sorely missed. While the other boys had fathers who attended their games, I didn't. There was no one there to break up the fights between my sister and my mother, except me, who they would then turn their attention to and I would become public enemy number one."

"Sounds like a dysfunctional family."

The man laughed. "Definitely. Sometimes I think my insomnia is linked to the two of them."

"Well, my son won't have a father to remember. Only a mother, and frankly, I'd be just as pleased if it was a girl. But whatever I get, I'm going to love that child with all my heart."

And protect it as much as she could.

"Why are you so obsessed with having children?"

That was such a personal question, and she couldn't answer it.

It had been the absolute worst time of her life.

No one to help her, except her friends.

Since then, she felt like she was chasing an elusive dream of what she'd lost. Time to leave and let this man believe what he wanted about her. Standing, she walked to the door.

As she pulled the door open and started inside, she heard him.

"You should find a man to marry first," he said. "You need a husband."

Oh, that was it. He must be one of those people who believed families were only between married people. Well, good for him, and she'd tried so hard to find a loving partner to start a life and family with. But it ended in ruin.

"No, I don't. I've tried life that way and it's not happening. So I'm going to do things my way now. No husband need apply. Just a turkey baster and a doctor. Good night."

Walking into the cabin, she slammed the door shut. Why was she letting an unknown man upset her? She didn't need men. She was done. Now everything that happened in her life was up to her. No one else. And especially not a man who was a complete stranger.

CHAPTER 4

*T*wo weeks later, Crystal went to see her gynecologist. After the exam, the doctor smiled at her.

"Everything looks great. Any other questions?"

Sitting up on the edge of the table with the sheet draped across her legs, she licked her lips. "Yes, I want to get pregnant."

"Great, you're running out of time," she said.

"I know. I'm not married and I have no one in my life. I'd like to do donor insemination. How do I get started?"

Sitting on her stool, the doctor sat back and gazed at her. "You can go online and research finding a sperm donor. You choose one and have the sperm sent here to the office and then we can do the procedure, which isn't difficult."

That sounded so easy.

"Or I know a man who is searching for a woman to have his child. His situation is unique and if you're interested, I can arrange a meeting between the two of you."

It would be nice to know something about the sperm

donor's background and to say she'd met him, but…"I don't want someone who wants to be a part of the child's life."

The doctor grimaced. "Understand and I don't think he does. He mainly wants to leave a part of himself here in this world. He's not in a position to raise a child."

That seemed odd. Did he have no money? Was that why he was not in a position to raise a child?

"I can't tell you much about him because of laws, but he's one of the nicest men I know, and his is a special case."

That intrigued her.

"Give him my name and tell him that I want to have a child, but I want very little attachment with the father. I don't expect child support or even visitation. Oh, and I'd like to know his medical background. What kind of diseases run in his family."

One good thing about meeting the father, she could form her own impressions of him. Her biggest fear was fathering the child of a psychopath. This way she could get to know him a little better than just a tube of sperm sent from a clinic.

A week later, the doctor called her.

"Crystal, he wants to meet you at a restaurant at three p.m. today. Will that work for you?"

An excited tingle spiraled through her. She glanced at her watch. That was two hours from now.

"Yes," she said. "But how will I know who he is?"

"He's getting the two of you a private room at the restaurant, so you can talk without someone overhearing you."

"Excellent," she said. "I'm so excited."

"Just be careful," the doctor said. "He's a good man but consider everything before you make a decision."

"Of course," she said, knowing she couldn't let her excitement cause her to make another bad choice. She had so many questions for him and she needed to sit down right now and make out a list.

The biggest question was why he was doing this.

Two hours later, she got out of her Mustang convertible and walked toward the restaurant.

When she entered the exclusive diner, she walked to the maître d.

"I'm meeting my party in the Surf Room," she said, thinking the name seemed way too casual for the fancy restaurant.

"Right this way," he told her.

Her hands shook and she felt so nervous, but then she realized she could always go back to plan A, which was to use an unknown sperm donor.

But there was something about knowing the father of her child that made her feel better.

She walked into the room and a handsome sandy-haired man was sitting at a table, scrolling on his phone. He glanced up and immediately stood.

"Hello," he said.

"Hello," she replied as he pulled out a chair for her.

"Can we keep this on a first-name basis for now?" he asked.

Why didn't he want her to know his last name?

"Sure," she replied. "I'm Crystal."

He smiled. "David. If this works out, then we can tell our last names, but I'm trying to keep this very quiet."

That was completely understandable. Especially after she'd spoken to the jerk on the cruise ship.

She gripped his hand. "It's nice to meet you and I'm going

to ask for one thing – we be completely honest with one another. If I'm not who you're looking for, then we'll shake hands and say have a nice life."

His blue eyes danced and he nodded. "Agree. So why are you doing this?"

There was so much she could say, but she wasn't certain how much she should tell him, so she'd start with the basics.

"For twenty years, since I graduated college, I've been searching for the 'right' man to marry. After three failed engagements, I'm giving up. I'm alone. Having a family is so important to me and I can't wait any longer. I'm thirty-eight and any day now I fear it won't be possible."

His head tilted and he gazed at her. "What do you mean you're alone?"

"My family died when I was in college. I have some distant aunts and uncles, but I've not heard from them. My closest friends are my family."

"So no men in your life now?"

"No, I was supposed to get married almost a month ago, but I broke off the engagement, went on the honeymoon cruise, and decided it was time to go after the family I want. Tell me why you're doing this."

With a sigh, he looked away and then back at her.

"I'm forty-eight years old and I have waited too late to get married and have the life I wanted. For too many years, I put my career first and now I'm alone. I'm in no position to raise a child myself. I'd like to see him or her whenever possible, but the actual raising of the child would be up to you. I'm not going to be there most of the time."

That seemed vague. Like he wanted to see them, but he wouldn't be there for any big events in the child's life.

"So you wouldn't interfere with me raising this child?"

"No," he said. "It's important to me that I leave something of myself behind on this earth. If I'm still here in ten or twenty years and the child wants to see me, I'm open to that. But I will not be there for the everyday raising of this child."

She still felt a little baffled and wondered why this was so important to him.

"You look confused," he said.

"I'm just wondering why you're doing this if you don't want to be in their everyday life. What if I decided seeing you was harmful for the child and I put an end to your seeing him or her?"

"I want what's best for the child. So if seeing me is harmful, then we can discuss why and if I agree with you, I'll have to live by your decision."

It just seemed too perfect.

"You realize that I don't expect child support or any kind of monetary compensation," she said.

He nodded. "Yes, the doctor told me."

"There are some questions I need to ask you," she said. "What are the health issues in your family."

Shaking his head, he shrugged a shoulder. "Not much. When we get older there is some dementia, arthritis, and a couple of cases of pancreatic cancer."

That was a little concerning. She would need to do some research on that cancer. But most people didn't get it until later in life.

"All right," she said. "That doesn't sound too bad. No schizophrenia? How about drug abuse? Have you ever used illegal drugs?"

"In college, but not since. How about you? Anything I need to know about?"

She laughed. "No drugs. I don't even like to drink too much," she said, remembering the night she consumed the entire bottle of champagne and how she suffered because of her stupidity.

"Look, I will promise you this. Already I'm trying to prepare my body for pregnancy. I'm eating right, exercising, and not taking any alcohol or prescription medicine of any kind. Doctor Jane gave me a whole book on pregnancy."

A smile spread across his face. "She's a friend of mine. That's how she knew I was searching for a birth mother."

"I really like her," Crystal said. "I have another question for you. If we move forward with this, I want a contract drawn up between us. In this contract, you have to agree that you will never sue me for custody of the baby. This child will be mine."

Gazing at her, he nodded. "Agreed. But in the contract, there must be a clause about who will take care of the child if something were to happen to you. I'm not going to have my child go into foster care."

That was something to consider. She had never thought of that and she liked that he brought it up.

"I'm agreeable to that. I'll have to ask one of my friends if she would take on the responsibility of raising the child."

She liked that he was thinking of the welfare of the baby. That made her feel good.

They had been talking for almost thirty minutes. She liked his easygoing manner.

"Tell me about yourself," she said. "I would like to know some things about you and your temperament."

A chuckle came from him. "I'm considered an introvert, a

hard worker, and yet my friendships are few and close. I'm not a party person, and in fact, I go to parties for just a little bit, and then I disappear and go home back to my sanctuary where I love to read, watch movies, and entertain a few close friends.

"In school, I did very well. I'm considered to have very high intelligence, but I'm not a genius by any means. The most disappointing aspect of my life is my relationships. I'm not good and women get frustrated with me."

She laughed. "Sounds like we have the same problems."

"What about you?"

"I'm flirty and fun, and years ago, I was the life of the party, but not anymore. Since college, I've settled down. Life kind of forced that on me and while I can still get crazy, just not like I used to. Since I own my own business, the baby will always be right there by my side. Most of the time, I work out of my home. I've got four incredibly close good friends. Men, I've given up on. I'm not interested in dating any longer. Like I said before, I'm alone. No real family."

For a moment, he sat staring at her and frowning.

"No DUIs?"

"Oh no," she said shaking her head. "Never. When I say crazy, my friends say I can become goofy and fun. I don't see it."

He laughed. "We never do see things about ourselves."

"No," she responded.

"So who would our child play with?"

That was a difficult question since she had no brothers or sisters. Even her friends and their children were almost grown. She'd waited so long to do this.

"When he's old enough, I'll be sending him to preschool

where he can learn to play with other children. It's important that I start that at a young age, to acquaint him with others."

"But no family members?"

"Nope, not a one left here on the island with me. Not a one," she said sighing. The pain of their loss still sat like a rock on her chest and she feared it always would.

For a few minutes, they both sat across from each other, the sound of dishes clanging together coming from the restaurant's kitchen.

Staring at him, she wondered if the baby would have his good looks. The sandy hair that he combed over to the side, his forehead was wide, and his nose was straight. High cheekbones and long lashes fluttered over his big blue eyes. Boy or girl, with his looks, they would be gorgeous.

"What do you think?" he said. "Should we progress and meet again or do you want to just shake hands and walk out of here?"

She felt so nervous. He seemed like a really nice guy. And she couldn't see any manipulation on his part. But she still had questions. She wanted to think on this some more.

"I'm willing to go forward. I'd like to meet again and bring my lawyer," she said. "Because he will think of things I've not considered."

The man grinned at her.

"Agree. And I'd like to bring mine as well. Do you mind me asking a personal question?"

"No," she said. "What?"

"When does your next cycle begin? If we're going to do this, the sooner the better," he said softly.

A shiver went through her as reality seemed to hit her.

"My most fertile period will be in two weeks. You really are in a hurry."

"Yes, I am," he said, standing.

Knowing the meeting was over, she stood as well.

"David Avara," he said. "I'm going to trust you to keep what we've spoken about today quiet. If I learn that you have spoken to anyone about this meeting, then the deal is off."

She kind of laughed. "Well, we haven't signed a contract yet. I'm going to tell my girlfriends what I'm doing, but I will not mention your name. No one will know who the father is but me and the child."

He sighed and she could tell he was relieved. She'd never heard of David Avara and she wondered if she should have.

"Crystal Young," she said.

He nodded. "I will confess, I knew your last name, Dr. Jane told me, but I asked that she not reveal my name."

"She didn't," she said.

"How long before we can meet with our lawyers? I'm serious that I would like for us to get pregnant in the next two weeks."

Just the thought of this happening so quickly made her anxious and excited. This was her dream.

"I'll contact my attorney this afternoon," she said. "Day after tomorrow?"

"I'll contact mine and then I'll get in touch with you," he said. "That is if you'll give your number."

"Of course," she said and pulled out her business card.

"We'll talk soon," he said and escorted her to the door. Once there, he turned and went back through the kitchen.

That was odd. Did he not want people to see him in the restaurant?

CHAPTER 5

*F*inding out you have months to live, really sucked. As in *why the hell do I deserve this* kind of suck.

There had been so few symptoms. Nothing out of the ordinary until jaundice sent him fleeing to the doctor to find out what was wrong. Who sent him to a specialist, who ran all kinds of tests and then delivered the bad news.

Pancreatic cancer stage four.

As much as he fought this disease, he knew the odds. And suddenly he realized his company would have no one except for his lawyer. No one to keep it running, to inherit it, no one. While he'd been busy building his empire, he'd forgotten one very important detail in life.

An heir. Someone to inherit the things he'd built. It was his own damn fault for working too hard to accomplish something with his life. And he'd been very successful. But now that he was going to leave this planet to the next generation, what good was everything he'd done?

He didn't even have a close niece or nephew. No one. Just like Crystal, and he'd felt her loneliness, understood why she wanted a family of her own. And he could help give her what she wanted. Plus, she would be giving him peace. He could die knowing there was a small part of him left here on earth who would inherit everything he'd worked for.

Only problem, she had no idea who he was or how rich he was. And until the deal was finalized, he didn't want her to know.

Being sick drained him and that short, stressful meeting with Crystal had worn him out. It didn't take much these days. The cancer doctor wanted to start chemotherapy right away and he was agreeable to try. But he wanted to make certain his sperm was not contaminated, so he made three deposits of sperm at the Cryobank. They promised him it would be all right, but he was waiting until he had a woman pregnant before he began the treatment.

Sitting on the couch, he picked up his phone and dialed the number.

"Hey, can you come over, we need to talk," he said.

"About damn time. Are you going to tell me what's going on?"

He chuckled.

"Yes," he said. "And bring over a large meat lovers pizza."

He'd pay dearly for eating so much grease, but right now, he was being good to himself by enjoying the foods he loved. Sooner or later, he would probably have to give them up.

"I'm on my way," he said.

The first year his company made a million dollars, he'd hired the best law firm in Corpus Christi. They kept sending out lawyers until one walked in and told him that he was going to be sued if he didn't fix the flooring in the front office. He'd found his man. Direct, honest, and to the point.

Leaning back, he closed his eyes and thought about Crystal. First thing he wanted done was a background check. Why was she alone? What happened to her family? Also, he wanted to know as much as possible about her engagements. The woman was a stunner and what man would walk away from her? Then he wanted to know about her zaniness. How far did she let that go before she got into trouble?

If she was smart, she would have her lawyer run a background check on him. And then the first thing they would do was sign a confidentiality report. No one should learn of his predicament.

When and if he died, he wanted it to be a shock to the gaming world.

Right now, even his lawyer didn't know.

Crystal wasn't the first woman he'd interviewed to have his child, but she was the best candidate to date. Now if only her background held up, then she would be the one. And God willing, he wanted to live to see his son or daughter born. That was all he asked for. Just to see that they arrived safely into this world, hold them, and say good-bye.

The doorbell rang and Maria, his housekeeper answered.

Soon, Tyler bound into the living area.

"Hey, man, how are you?"

"Great," he said.

"How was the cruise?"

He laughed. "Other than my mother and sister fighting for two days and then meeting this crazy woman at midnight, it was great."

"I told you it wasn't a good idea to share a suite with your mother and sister. That there would be trouble."

"You were right," he said, sinking down into a chair.

"And you picked up a woman at midnight? I thought those days were over," he said.

"No, I didn't pick her up. She was in the cabin next to ours and I had to help her out of her wedding dress. She threw a negligee and her wedding dress overboard and she got drunk on champagne."

David laughed. "You have the most interesting experiences when you travel."

"She was crazy," he said. "Batshit crazy."

They sat there in comfortable silence for a few moments.

"Maria is going to put the pizza in the oven for a few minutes and then she'll bring it out to us," he said.

"Good, I'm hungry," David said. "Had an interesting afternoon myself."

Tyler's brows rose. "Are you going to tell me what's going on with you? I know something is on your mind. You've been acting strange."

David sighed. How did you tell someone you were dying and ask them to keep it quiet? That you would like to die in peace without the television cameras just waiting for the news of your demise.

"I've had some back pain recently and then it moved into my abdomen. I still wasn't too concerned, but then I turned yellow. And that freaked me out. So I went to the doctor."

Tyler's expression changed to concern and his brown eyes gazed at him with worry.

"What did they find?"

"I have stage four pancreatic cancer," he said still not really believing those words. Yes, he felt bad, but not all the time. Yes, he was tired, sometimes nauseous and he'd lost some weight, but not how he would expect to feel dying.

Tyler leaned back against his chair and rubbed his hand over his face.

"No," he said. "No, you can't die on me."

"I will start chemotherapy next week. We'll see how the cancer reacts to the chemo. It's too late to do surgery, so this is my only hope."

Tyler looked at the ceiling, his eyes watering. They were friends and clients, they had worked together for years. He tried to put himself in his position and how he would feel.

He would be devastated.

Tyler stood and paced the room.

"There has to be something. Some specialist somewhere in the world that can help you."

He'd thought the same thing when he first learned of his disease.

"I've already sought out a second opinion and even traveled to MD Anderson Cancer Center."

"Why didn't you tell me? I would have gone with you," he said, stopping to stare at him. "How long have you known?"

"Only about a month. But you were busy with the oil heiress case. I couldn't interfere and ask you to go with me."

"You damn sure could," he said. "You know I would have made time for you."

"And then you were going on that eightieth birthday cruise with your mother and I didn't want to spoil it. You have a family, I don't. So I need to let you know of some decisions I've made."

David could see Tyler's legal mind taking over and knew

he was going to give him hell on what he'd decided, but it was his decision and no one else's.

"You're not dying," Tyler said. "We're going to find a doctor who knows how to cure this."

If only there was one. Some people lived for years with this, but some didn't.

"Let me tell you what I've realized in the last month."

Maria brought the pizza into the den and they both just looked at it, all pretense of being hungry gone.

"Maria, bring my friend a beer. I think he needs one," David said, seeing how white Tyler's face was. It was slowly starting to sink in that he could die. Just like it had slowly sunk in for David.

"Yes, sir," she said and hurried to the kitchen. In a moment, she came back with the canned beverage.

"Thank you," Tyler said to the woman before he turned his attention back to David.

"In this last month, I've realized what I've given up by working so hard to make this company a success. Without a wife or children, I have no one to leave it to. With a sister that wouldn't know what to do with the company or anyone else, I didn't know what to do with the business. Sell it? But then what? No, I want to leave my company to my son or daughter. But I don't have a son or daughter and time is running out."

Tyler picked up a piece of pizza and began to devour it. He did this when his mind was churning and he was thinking about how to fix a problem.

"It's not too late for me to get someone to have my child. But I won't be here to watch over them, so I contacted my good friend, Dr. Jane, who runs an OB/GYN clinic here on the island and told her what I was looking for."

"No, you're not going to do this," Tyler said. "It's much too dangerous."

"I've already interviewed three women. Two of them were completely wrong. They were too young, married, or just not right. Then yesterday, I met a young woman named Crystal and I like her. I like her a lot. We have a lot in common. We have no one. We're alone."

Tyler shook his head. "No, there are so many dangerous legal pitfalls. What if she's on drugs? What if she's not a good mother? What if she marries and your son or daughter is raised by some crackhead?"

David had thought these same thoughts. And he was afraid, but he also wanted this so badly, he could imagine himself holding that small bundle of joy in his arms before he died. This was his last chance.

"You're right and that's where I need you to be the legal eagle you've always been."

Tyler all but stuffed a piece of pizza in his mouth, he would probably have indigestion later because of the way he was nervously consuming pizza. The smell had been enough for David. At first, he'd loved it, but now it was starting to make him feel that icky sick feeling that let him know, no pizza for him.

And definitely no alcohol.

"I'm going to tell you right up front that I'm against this. But if you're insistent on doing this, we need a concrete contract that lets the mother know if she does anything wrong, she will lose this child. I will take over the raising of it myself, if need be. I will fight her in court and make certain your child is well protected."

Immense relief filled David. This was what he loved about

Tyler. About his friendship and legal mind. He was a protective soul that would make certain Crystal did her part in raising his child.

Pulling out her card, he handed it to him. "We're meeting with her the day after tomorrow. Draw up the contracts and do a background check on her. Make certain everything is in place when we meet with her and her lawyer."

Tyler sighed. He stopped eating and leaned back and drank from his beer.

"Did you tell her you had pancreatic cancer?"

"No, she doesn't even know who I am unless she went home and looked me up on the internet. She is not to be told I have cancer until we can't keep it from her any longer."

Maybe that was being deceitful, but his fear was that the world would learn that he was dying, and if it was his time to go, he wanted to die in peace.

"This sucks," Tyler said. "You were supposed to find the perfect girl of your dreams, get married, and start a family."

And now it would not happen.

"Yes, well, I waited too long. Just like you're waiting too long. Get out there and find someone. You don't want to wake up one morning and learn that your time here has just reached an expiration date."

Though he hoped he had many more years left, but the stats were not good. Especially when they talked about palliative care. Some people survived, and he hoped and prayed that he would be one of them. But so many didn't.

Time to get his affairs in order.

"After we get this contract signed and she's pregnant, then we'll talk about my last wishes."

Tyler ran his hands over his face. "No. You're going to beat this. We can talk about your last wishes, but you're not going to die."

David wished that was true. But he couldn't be certain.

CHAPTER 6

*C*rystal was as nervous as a cat going to the vet's office. This was the day they would sign the paperwork if everything seemed right. Her lawyer walked by her side.

"I hope like hell you know what you're doing," he said.

"You did the background check," she said.

"Oh, yes," he replied. "Do you know who this man is?"

"No, someone who wants a baby just like I do," she said.

"He's David Avara, owner of DA Gaming Systems. Wealthy beyond belief. He could marry anyone he wanted and have a child. Why is he doing it this way?"

Why did lawyers always make everything about money?

"Well, I don't want his money," she said. "And I accepted his reasons for wanting a child. You did put in the contract that he cannot seek custody of this child."

"I did, but he has enough money, he could buy the jury, the judge, and anyone else fighting him to get custody. You have to realize he can outgun you in the legal department."

For some reason, she wasn't afraid of David, though she

would watch him carefully. There seemed to be an air of sadness about him.

Clint, her lawyer, opened the door to the restaurant.

The man waved them on back and they headed for the Sand Cove room. She needed to remember this and write it down in a baby book about how she met the baby's father in a restaurant.

David was waiting for them, but he appeared pale and even nervous.

Walking over to her, he kissed her on the cheek. "Crystal," he said.

"David, this is my lawyer Clint Edwards," she said.

"Nice to meet you," Clint said and backed away.

"All we're missing is my lawyer," David said. "He's perpetually late."

"With good reason," a voice she remembered said.

Whirling around, she felt her mouth drop open before she gasped. "You."

In the light of the restaurant, the man was incredibly handsome. Dark hair with bushy dark brows, and sparkling white teeth framed by a mouth that was luscious and so kissable. He had a straight nose and high cheekbones with big emerald eyes that had long dark sweeping eyelashes.

Why was he still single?

"Yes, me, and I'm going to do my best to talk my friend and client out of doing this. You're a crazy woman," he said.

She tensed and lowered her voice. "When I met you, I had good reason to be a little crazy."

David sighed. "Everyone, sit down and let's talk this out. It's obvious you two know each other."

"No, we don't," Crystal said. "We spoke in the dark on the balcony of a cruise ship. We never introduced ourselves."

"Tyler Nelson, attorney of law," he said, holding out his hand.

God, she wanted to push it away but knew that would look mean and petty.

"Crystal Young, sane, intelligent woman who owns her own business and will soon have her own family."

He laughed.

"And this is my lawyer, Clint Edwards," she said.

"Hi, Clint," Tyler said.

Oh dear God, they knew each other too.

They all sat at a small round table. The lights were dim in the room and she turned them up. "Now, I can see to read your contract," she said.

"Bad eyesight," Tyler said, writing it down.

"No, good eyesight, but you're not going to slip something by me."

Tyler grinned like that was the opening he needed.

"I'm advising my client, to not walk, but run from you. You are not a good candidate to have this man's child."

"Tell me your reasons," she said.

"You were drunk on the ship, you sat out on the deck in your bra and panties, and you told me six nights later that you were going to do this. You also told me that you had been engaged three times and been a three-time loser."

The man thought he was telling things to David that he didn't know, but he knew most of that.

"You have insomnia. You've not been in love since high school. You fight with your mother and sister, so would that make you a bad father?"

Shaking his head, his mouth turned up in a dangerous smile. No matter what, she was not going to let him rile her. She would fight for what she wanted.

"I wasn't drunk," he said.

"You had not run away from a wedding either. As for sitting out on the deck in my bra and panties, you unhooked my wedding dress for me and since I felt like you had already seen my underwear, I would just sit there and finish off that bottle of celebratory champagne for a wedding that didn't happen."

David laughed. "If I had run away from a wedding, I would probably get drunk as well."

"Did I proposition you? Did I make any advances toward you? Did I come on to you in any kind of way," she asked Tyler.

With a sigh, he shook his head. "No."

"And I would have knocked you down if you had tried anything. If you recall, I told you I was done with men. And I still am. David wants a child and I want a child. So why don't you stick to your lawyer duties and let's get through this."

"You're just after his money," he said.

She laughed. "Honey, I don't need his money. Now read the contract."

David snickered and Tyler was growing more and more agitated. Clint handed Tyler and David a copy of their contract. "Here is our proposal. As you can see on page three, we put in a clause that says Mr. Avara does not have to pay child support."

Tyler glared at her and she gave him her best smile.

"Visitation rights are on page four, and mainly we just ask

that he notify Miss Young within twenty-four hours and that the visits not be overnight."

There was silence for a moment and then Tyler said, "We'll want to discuss that provision."

"No, it's all right," David said. "I couldn't keep a baby or even a toddler overnight. I wouldn't know how to take care of them. Did you make provisions for who would take care of the child if something happens to you?"

This one had been hard.

"As you know, I have no family left. So my friend Nicole Clark, who has five children, said she would take the baby. But I also wanted to give you the opportunity to raise the child first. So you're the first person and Nicole is second."

David smiled at her. "Thank you. That's what I needed to know."

Turning in his chair, Tyler gazed at David, but didn't say anything.

How in the world had she managed to pick the one person whose lawyer was Tyler Nelson, the jerk she met on the boat?

"Is there anything else?" Clint asked.

"I need a private word with my client," Tyler said.

The two of them got up and walked to a corner. She could see Tyler trying so hard to convince him that this wasn't a good idea. That she wasn't worthy enough to have his child.

David shook his head and his mouth formed the word no and then he turned and walked back to the table.

Tyler had been outvoted.

"You're sure you want to do this?" David said, gazing at her.

"More than anything. You're giving me back what I've been missing," she said.

"And you're giving me an heir," he said smiling.

Her heart fluttered in her chest and she felt at peace with the decision.

Clint had been reading the contract and he handed it to her. "It looks good."

She smiled and he handed her a pen. Quickly she signed her name to it.

Tyler had returned to the table, and he finished reading their contract.

"I think this is a terrible idea. I don't think that Miss Young is the right person to be the mother of your child, but the contract looks good."

David smiled at her, picked up the pen, and quickly signed the document.

"When can we start?"

"I've already made an appointment with Dr. Jane and we're hoping to do the insemination next week," she said, tears filling her eyes.

She was going to be a mom. She was going to get the family she'd dreamed of, though without a husband.

"You'll let me know how it goes?" David said.

"Of course," she said. "How much do you want to be involved?"

"I'm excited," he said. "As much as you feel comfortable with."

She smiled. "David, because of you, I'm going to be a mom. I'll keep you informed as to what's going on."

"Could I be there when you go back to see if the insemination took?"

"Yes," she said. "I think that would be wonderful for us to learn at the same time."

He grinned and her lawyer smiled.

"I've got another meeting I need to get to," he said.

"Me too," Tyler said with a sigh, shaking his head. "Can't believe I couldn't talk you out of this. Either one of you."

Standing, she came around the table and hugged David. "Thank you. I'm so excited. We'll talk soon."

She glanced at Tyler and smiled. The man was so damn handsome and stubborn, and she wanted to punch him but knew that wouldn't be good.

"Good-bye, Tyler, I'm sure you'll be around. Probably couldn't get rid of you if I tried."

"You're damn right I'm going to be around to make certain you don't take advantage of my client," he said.

"Did you do a background check on me?"

"Yes," he said. "I don't believe it."

She smiled. "You should."

CHAPTER 7

*A*lready Crystal was learning that getting pregnant was going to be more nerve-racking than it appeared. When she called the doctor, they had lined her up for an ultrasound and then her doctor gave her a *trigger shot* that would cause a mature egg to release, and they scheduled the implantation two days after that. That simple procedure had brought tears to her eyes.

The fact that the child she longed for could be created at that moment made her joyous and happy and tearful all at the same time. Dr. Jane had told her that was common and to cry away.

While she lay there, she thought of all the things she would need to do before the baby was born. And she grew even more excited to think that in nine months, she would have a son or daughter. Someone to love. A family.

Fourteen days later, she returned to the clinic, a big bundle of nerves. Today, they were doing a blood test before she and David were scheduled to meet with the doctor and learn the results.

A blood test that would reveal whether or not she was pregnant.

For the last two weeks, she'd been cautious, eaten right, and done everything she thought an expectant mother should do. But they didn't know if the egg and the sperm had connected and implanted in her uterus.

If her HCG levels were high, then she was pregnant. If not, then the treatment had failed.

"As soon as we have the results, the doctor will speak to you," the nurse said, putting tape and a cotton ball over the place she'd withdrawn blood. "You can sit in the waiting room."

"Thank you," she said, her nerves strung tighter than the horsehair strings on a violin.

In the waiting room, she glanced at the pregnant women and prayed that someday soon she would join their ranks. How many of them had gone to such lengths to get pregnant?

With a sigh, she hoped that David would arrive before they called her back. It was odd that he wasn't here. He'd been checking on her every day. When they last spoke, he'd told her he would be here.

The waiting room was quiet, most of the women flipping the pages of a magazine while they waited.

Her stomach tightened with fear and she didn't know how she was going to handle the news if she wasn't pregnant. What if she couldn't have a baby? What if they did this three times and nothing happened?

Tyler came charging through the door into the waiting room, his shoes squeaking on the floor as he approached her and sank down beside her.

"Sorry, I'm late," he said.

The man wore a suit that made him look like he should be on the cover of a magazine. Quickly he reached up and loosened the tie before he removed it and crammed it into his pocket. Losing the tie didn't make him look any less attractive. He ran a hand through his dark hair and sighed.

"Just got out of court," he said. "I was beginning to think I wasn't going to be here."

If she were still interested in men, she might have toyed with him a little bit, but not now. Not when she was trying to create her dream.

"Where's David? I thought he was coming," she said, wishing it was him instead of Tyler.

This man didn't approve of her or of what they were doing. She took a deep breath and a woodsy scent filled her nostrils. He smelled so good, she almost wanted to lick him. But she wouldn't. He appeared more like a handsome banker, though he acted like a lawyer.

"He's not feeling well and didn't want to take a chance on exposing you or the baby or the pregnant women here," he said, glancing around. "Damn, there's a lot of pregnant women in this room."

"You're sitting in a gynecologist/obstetrician's office," she said. "That's what Dr. Jane does for a living. You're the odd one in here."

He gave her a smirk.

"Aren't we touchy today," he said.

"Yes, my nerves are shot, and I wanted David beside me, not you," she said.

With a sigh, she tried to lean back and take deep, calming breaths.

"Don't you think it's a little odd that you and my best

friend and boss are now creating a child together? We didn't even exchange names on the boat. How did you find out about him," he asked. "I never revealed anything about David and yet here you are."

This man didn't want to believe this happened by accident. He thought she had deliberately sought out David. Taking a deep breath, she reminded herself that she needed to stay calm.

"Sorry to ruin your suspicions. Dr. Jane gave him my first name and phone number. I didn't contact him, he contacted me," she said. "I didn't even know who he was until Clint told me about him. I don't play video games."

Shaking his head, he looked straight ahead. "That just seems so impossible."

"Maybe fate intervened," she said. "Believe me, I know your feelings on this and would never have involved you. In fact, you can leave right now and that would be fine."

He chuckled. "No, I'm here looking out for my client's best interest. He's so excited about this baby. And if you hurt him, I will come after you."

"Threats?"

"Promises," he said.

"He's giving me what I want, why would I come after him?"

"Because people do all the time. He has money. They sue."

"Sorry, to disappoint you, but I'm not going to sue him," she said, remembering how she'd sued once before and the pain associated with that trial.

The man's threats made no sense. They had a contract and she planned on fulfilling her part, if she could. Besides, she liked David. He was kind to her. He acted like he cared about her. When she spoke to David, he always asked how she was feeling and if there had been any signs yet that she was pregnant. And sadly, there was nothing.

"David seems like a wonderful man," she said. "I'm honored that he's the father of my child. You can take your suspicions right on down the hall. I don't need them."

"Not going anywhere."

Tyler didn't say anything more and she knew he didn't like the fact she hoped she was carrying David's child.

"What happens if you're not pregnant?"

"I don't want to talk about it," she said, picking up a magazine and flipping through it. "Let's not jinx it, shall we."

Deep, slow breaths, she reminded herself.

The door to the inside offices opened. "Crystal."

Oh my, this was it. Soon she would learn if the insemination had worked and if she was pregnant. Her knees shook as she stood and walked toward the nurse. Sadly, Tyler was right behind her.

"Follow me," the woman said and Tyler took Crystal's elbow.

Neither of them said a word as the nurse led them into the doctor's office.

"Have a seat," Dr. Jane said. They sat and she sighed. Not a good sign. "I'm sorry to tell you, that you're not pregnant. Unfortunately, the insemination didn't take," she said.

Tears welled in Crystal's eyes. She couldn't stop them. Disappointment and hurt filled her and Dr. Jane handed her a tissue.

"It's all right. This is our first attempt and now we know it's not going to be as easy as we hoped. How do you feel about taking fertility drugs? There is a chance you could have more than one baby, but they will also ramp up your egg production."

"No," Tyler said. "We only want one baby."

"Who are you," Dr. Jane asked.

"I'm David's attorney," he said. "He couldn't be here today because he's ill."

The doctor sighed. "This decision is going to be Crystal's. No one else."

Crystal was so sad, so disappointed that she was willing to try anything if she thought it would help.

"Let's do it," she said.

"Good, I think it will help and the risk of multiple babies is low on the drug I'm going to prescribe. You start taking them on the first day of your cycle. Again, we'll do a sonogram to see if your eggs are maturing about a week before your ovulation time. Then I'll probably give you another trigger shot. Call us and let's set this up as soon as you start your cycle."

Crystal sat there feeling so defeated. Maybe her dream wasn't possible.

"What if I can't get pregnant?"

"No, let's not worry about that just yet. This is the first attempt and I will tell you that it normally takes more than one try. You're healthy and your eggs look good. Something just didn't connect. We'll try again. Now I want you to go home, relax, and not worry about this. I feel confident this is going to work. If this month the fertility drugs don't work, we'll try a stronger one next month."

With a heavy heart, she stood.

"Thank you, I won't give up hope," she said.

"Of course not. We're going to get you pregnant," Dr. Jane said. "Now I'll see you in two to three weeks."

They walked out of the office and down a hall where they stepped into the elevator. The tears started to flow and she couldn't contain them any longer. They ran down her face and sobs racked her body. It just wasn't fair. She wanted a baby so badly.

Tyler wrapped his arm around her and held her while she sobbed.

"I know I shouldn't be crying, but I was so hopeful. So excited and had even started trying to figure out the date of the baby's birth," she sobbed. "I just want my own family."

The elevator doors opened and Tyler wrapped his arm around her waist and led her outside into the parking lot.

"I'm sorry this time didn't work out, but it sounds promising," he said.

She gave a little laugh. "Yes, it does and I know I should just relax and think maybe next month. But I'm disappointed."

He took her in his arms again and the strangest feeling overwhelmed her. It felt good to be held by him. There was a sense of peace, of belonging, of him caring she was hurting, and yet they could never be. She was done with men and he hated what she was doing.

"You're going to try again. I know David is so excited about this child and I would hate for him to be disappointed at this stage."

That was an odd thing for him to say.

Stepping back, she wiped her eyes.

"Thank you. I'm going home, putting on my favorite movie, and eating takeout food," she said. "Maybe Chinese."

"Sounds like a perfectly boring evening."

"It will be. Do you want me to call David or are you going to tell him?" she asked.

"I'm going over there now," he said. "I want to check on him and make certain he's all right."

"You two aren't..." How did she ask the question she needed an answer to? After her last experience, she wasn't taking any chances on not knowing the truth about someone. David and Tyler were close, but how close were they really?

"No," Tyler said. "We both like women. They just don't seem to like us too much."

She laughed.

"I don't understand why," he said.

"When we have time, I'll tell you," she said.

He grinned at her. "I just bet you would," he said.

She thought of how she had wanted to spend this evening calling her friends and telling them she was expecting. But it wasn't meant to be.

Tears welled in her eyes again.

"I've got to go," she said. "Tell David I'm sorry and that I hope next month will be better."

"You have nothing to be sorry for," he told her. "We'll try again. The doctor is optimistic."

With a sigh, she impulsively gave him a hug. Maybe she needed to feel his arms around her again or maybe it was her way of thanking him for being so caring when she received the bad news.

"Thank you. I'm glad someone was with me when I found out."

She released him and hurriedly walked to her car. Today, Tyler had shown her a different side of himself and she actually liked it. But it didn't matter. She was focused on getting pregnant.

CHAPTER 8

Tyler knew that David was going to be disappointed. The man had made him promise that he would tell him as soon as he left the doctor's office.

Today was the first time the chemotherapy had gotten to him. And Tyler feared there would be more days like this. He realized he would be the stand-in father whenever Crystal had a doctor's appointment and David couldn't attend.

Pulling up David's driveway, he glanced at the back of the mansion and how it cascaded down to the beach. While the house itself was not right on the water, there was a private beach area in the back that Tyler enjoyed.

And the house sat high enough that hopefully, the water would never wash it away, only a hurricane category four or higher could demolish the house.

After parking, he got out of the car and went inside.

"Hello, it's me, Tyler," he called not wanting to startle the maid or David.

"Back in the den," David called.

Walking to the back of the house, he saw his friend lying on the couch, with an IV in his arm.

A nice young woman was watching the drip.

"Tyler, this is Karen. She's my nurse," he said.

When had he gotten so bad that he needed a nurse?

"I'm just here giving him some fluids," she said. "The doctor determined he was dehydrated from being sick. Hopefully this will make him feel better. We're almost done."

Why did this feel like a slap in the face? Like a giant wake-up call. His friend was seriously ill and all he wanted to do was make him healthy again.

"Are you feeling better?"

"A little," he said. "Threw up my toenails, so at least that's stopped."

He glanced at David and then at the nurse, knowing his client and friend wouldn't want him to say anything in front of her. When you were as rich and famous as David, people talked. They liked to drop your name like you were the best of friends.

"How is Crystal?"

Tyler shook his head to let his friend know they shouldn't say anything else, even though he could see he was anxious to know.

"There we go," the nurse said. "All done. I'm going to take your vitals and then I'll be on my way. If you are still sick in the morning, call us."

She took his bio readings and then she packed up her equipment.

"Call us if you need us," she said, and Tyler walked her to the door.

"Is he all right?"

"He's fine. Just experiencing the side effects of the chemo-therapy. Feed him something light tonight."

"Thank you," Tyler said as she walked out the door.

With a heavy heart, he went back to where David lay resting.

"Can I get you anything?"

"No, you can sit your ass down and tell me what happened," he said. "I'm dying to know."

Already, Tyler had to deal with Crystal's disappointment and he hated that he had to tell his friend that the insemination didn't take.

"She's not pregnant," he said.

David sighed heavily and closed his eyes. "I just want to be here to see my son or daughter born. I'm running out of time."

Tyler tensed.

"No, you're going to beat this. You're going to be here and watch him grow. Don't give up on me."

David glanced away and Tyler could see he was so disappointed. "I hope you're right."

"Good. The doctor wasn't discouraged at all. In fact, she said that most of the time it doesn't take the first time. But she put Crystal on fertility drugs."

"Oh my goodness," David said with a laugh. "I just want one, not an entire baseball team."

"I said no, but the doctor said it was Crystal's decision. But the medication rarely causes multiple births. It mainly just increases egg production. So she is to start taking those when her cycle starts. And then in two weeks, they will try again."

Staring at him, David asked, "How did Crystal take the news."

"She cried. She was so disappointed. She cried in the

doctor's office, she cried in the elevator, and she cried in the parking lot."

"Is she okay?"

"I think so, she was just so disappointed," he said, remembering the look on her face when the doctor gave the news.

Now that he'd read her background report, he understood her need for her own family. When you'd lost everyone, it would be so hard every time there was a family holiday, having no one to share it with.

"How did you handle her tears," David asked.

"You'd be proud of me. I held her while she cried," he said, recalling the feel of her lush body against his. If only she wasn't involved with David.

Even on the boat, he'd been attracted to her and looked for her at every excursion, every meal, and every show, but she hadn't shown up.

That was where he would have liked to have gotten to know her better, not now, not like this. Not with her trying to get pregnant with his boss's child.

And yet, after learning her background and being around her more, he really did like her.

For everything she'd endured, she had to be a very strong woman.

"I'm going to send her flowers," David said, picking up his phone. "Maybe two dozen to cheer her up."

He dialed a local florist who knew him and Tyler listened to the conversation.

"I'll get those out to her right now," the woman said.

"Thank you, I know it's late, and I appreciate your help," David told the woman.

Without a doubt, the woman also knew that David would tip her handsomely.

"Am I crazy for doing this," David asked as he hung up the phone. "I just want a piece of me left here on this earth. A small part of myself."

Yes, Tyler thought he was crazy, but he knew all the ways this could go horribly wrong.

"As your lawyer, I have to tell you there are so many risks you're taking with this child. As your friend...I'm torn. You know my father was killed when I was young. It's hard on a son growing up in a house full of women."

David glanced at him. "Then I think you should step in as the boy's father."

"No, you're going to be here," Tyler said. "And besides, Crystal doesn't want anything to do with me. Our beginning was not too friendly."

His friend laughed and tried to sit up. Tyler was stunned at how weak he was. He'd always been so strong.

"It seems like you made some progress today if she let you comfort her," he said. "Maybe the real problem is that you're both attracted to one another."

"Oh, hell no," Tyler said as he realized he did like to look at her voluptuous body. Even that night on the ship, he'd enjoyed the view.

But the woman was crazy. Sure she came across as normal, but for her to throw her wedding gown overboard, breaking rules twice, that was wrong.

"Besides, her last engagement went bad because the guy was gay," Tyler said. "I don't think she knows how to find the right person."

"Then you could be perfect for her," David said, laughing.

"We've never found the perfect woman to marry. You should ask her out."

"Oh no," Tyler said. "You're my client and she's under contract with you. I could get into all kinds of legal entanglements. Besides, she's going to be pregnant soon."

Suddenly, David grabbed a bucket on the side of the couch, leaned over, and retched.

Damn, it was so hard to see his friend suffering like this. Tyler went to the kitchen and got him a glass of water and brought it back along with a wet cloth.

"Here," he said.

David sipped at the water and wiped his mouth. "I've got six more treatments of this and each one will get worse. I'm only on number two. By the end of this, I may be begging to die."

This was his worst nightmare and yet he couldn't abandon his friend. David lay back on the couch.

"How would you feel about a movie night? Your choice," he told him. "I'll stay the night and we can watch TV all night or until you fall asleep."

David chuckled. "Thanks, man, I know what you're doing. You're staying with me because you don't want me to be alone."

"True, but you do have the best sound system to watch movies and I'll ask Maria to make me some of her famous tacos unless you can't tolerate the smell of them."

With a sigh, David shook his head. "No, you eat tacos. I'm thinking nothing for now and maybe something light later when I can keep it down."

Six more chemotherapy treatments. Two more days of

being too weak to stand. How could his friend endure more treatments if they became worse than this?

"Plus, I can make certain you make it to the bathroom on your own. I don't think Maria believes that's in her job description."

"Probably not," David said.

"When is the next round of chemo?"

"In three weeks. Just about the time I start feeling better, they will hit me with another dose," he said, lying with his eyes closed.

His face was pale, and for the first time, Tyler realized he could very well lose his friend to this disease, and that hit him hard right in the chest.

No matter what happened, he was going to be right here at his side.

CHAPTER 9

*C*rystal was beginning to know Dr. Jane's office staff. When she walked in today, she smiled at the girl behind the counter.

"D-day," she said softly.

"Good luck," the girl said. "Have a seat and they'll call you back soon."

In just a few minutes, they led her to the back and the girl in the lab took her blood.

"I'll get this tested and then the doctor will see you," she said.

Crystal walked back to the waiting area and David was there looking for her. He looked pale and he'd lost weight. His sandy hair was still perfectly combed to the side, but there was a tiredness about him that she'd never noticed. Even his brown eyes appeared dull.

"David," she said and he turned toward her. After walking over to her, he kissed her on the cheek.

"How are you feeling?"

"Anxious," she said. "I want this so badly that I'm now

doing a meditation every day to make me relax and accept whatever happens. This has been way more stressful than I anticipated."

"I'm certain," he said and they both sat to await the doctor.

"You look like you've lost some weight," she said.

He nodded. "Yes, I've been working out a little and the weight just seemed to come off."

Just then, Tyler walked through the door.

"What's he doing here?" she asked frustrated at the sight of him. Yes, last time he had been incredibly supportive, but that didn't mean he had accepted what she was doing. And why his acceptance was important, she didn't know. His opinion meant nothing.

"My car is in the shop and he drove me here," David said. "But Tyler can stay in the waiting room if that makes you more comfortable."

"Yes," she said, not wanting him in there with them. Last time, it should have been David, but he'd been ill. From the way he looked right now, he didn't look much better.

These two seemed to always be together just like Aaron and Spencer, but Tyler had assured her they were not gay. Not that it would matter, she just liked to know who she was dealing with.

Just then the nurse came to the door. "Crystal."

Instinctively, she took David's hand. He looked down at her and smiled.

"Positive thoughts," he said.

"Yes," she replied.

They walked into the doctor's office and Dr. Jane smiled at David.

"Good to see you," she said.

He nodded to her. She waited until they were both seated.

"Good news. You're pregnant," she said, smiling.

Crystal felt her heart slam into her chest and she turned to David and they threw their arms around each other and hugged. If people saw them, they would think they were together, but they were only friends with a common interest.

Tears welled in her eyes and she started to cry.

Dr. Jane handed her a tissue just like last time.

"Happy tears," Crystal said.

"I think the fertility drugs were the trick we needed and now we have to watch you closely for the first few months. Not that I think you're going to have a difficult pregnancy, but my patients that have been waiting so long, I like to keep a close eye on them."

Crystal turned to David who was wiping the tears from his eyes. "We're having a baby."

"You're having the baby" he replied. "I'm just along for the ride and to watch your stomach grow each day with our child," he said. "I'm so excited. When is the baby due?"

"Looks like late October," she said. "He or she will be born this year."

David sighed and then reached out across the desk and shook her hand. "Thank you, Dr. Jane. Thank you so much."

She smiled at him. "Oh, David, I'm just thrilled for you and Crystal."

"Before you leave, the nurse is going to give you a pamphlet on being pregnant. We want you to know the warning signs of a miscarriage, but not worry about it. As much as this baby is wanted, I'm hoping for an easy pregnancy for you."

Crystal felt overwhelmed with emotion. She was pregnant.

Pregnant. Baby X would be born the end of October. All her dreams were coming true.

They stood.

"We'll see you in a month," the doctor said. "Call if you have any concerns. And, David, good to see you."

He nodded and they walked out of the office. They were both smiling and the nurses they passed grinned at them.

"Congratulations," one woman said. "Let's get you the paperwork and then you're good to go. Remember, don't hesitate to call us if you have any questions."

Tears filled her eyes again and she took the information from the nurse.

As they walked out the door, Tyler sat staring at his phone. He glanced up at them and they smiled.

"You're pregnant," he said.

"Yes," she replied, grinning. "We're having a baby in late October."

He stood and wrapped his arms around the two of them. "Congratulations," he said first to David and then to Crystal.

"Yes, I was against this, but now that we're having a baby, I'm thrilled for you."

Really? After everything he'd said on the boat, now he was congratulating them both. What had changed his mind?

"I think this calls for a celebration," David said. "Come on, we're going to the Luxx Club, my treat."

It was the fanciest restaurant in town and yet she didn't care. They had so much to celebrate.

"I'm driving both of you," Tyler said. "Especially since I know that Crystal drives a Mustang."

She grinned. "Yes, but I also have an SUV. But you're right, today I brought the Mustang so I could put the top down."

Even though it was early February, the weather had been unseasonably warm and she'd enjoyed tootling around the island with the sun on her face. It was her one luxury and once she got big and pregnant, it would be hard to get in and out of.

They all piled into the big SUV that Tyler drove.

"This is so much better than last month," Tyler said. "Last month I had to pick up both of you. But now we're celebrating a new life."

David didn't say much, but Crystal knew he was excited. Sitting in the doctor's office, he'd had tears in his eyes.

And how did he know Dr. Jane? It seemed like they were acquaintances. For a man who didn't intend to have much to do with this child, he seemed very interested.

When they reached the restaurant, they went inside and were immediately seated in a private room.

Sometimes she felt David and Tyler didn't want to be seen with her. They always seemed to prefer a private room. But then again, maybe it was because of David's fame. She still found it hard to believe he was worth billions and he'd never gotten married and had children.

Clint had given her his background check and she'd been shocked, but still she didn't care about his money, only his sperm. And it had worked.

Tyler ordered a bottle of champagne and David and she looked at him.

"No champagne," David said.

"No, alcohol of any kind," Crystal told him.

"Oh," Tyler said. "Sorry, I just thought we'd celebrate."

"And we will without alcohol," she told him. "In fact, I want a big appetizer and then I want steak."

The two men glanced at her and laughed.

"Are you going to be calling me, asking me to run to the store to satisfy a craving?" Tyler asked.

"No," she replied. "If I have a craving, I'll go get it myself. I'm quite capable of taking care of me and the baby."

David turned to her and took her hand. "But if you need something, you will call me. I realize you're very independent, but I'm here for you. This child is so important to me."

How had she found such a nice man to have a baby with? And why did it feel like he was always going to be in her life now? When this baby was born, she didn't think he could walk away and maybe that was for the best.

"Of course," she said, grinning at him. "We're going to be parents."

"Yes," David said and looked away.

For a moment, it looked like he was going to cry and she didn't understand what was going on.

Licking his lips, he turned toward her. "I have a request which you can deny me, that's your right. But I would really like it if the baby had my last name. Of course, the child would still be yours, but his name would be different. Would that be a problem?"

She thought about it for a moment. How could this negatively affect the child's life?

"You're well known."

"And we would not tell anyone that he or she is my child, but I think when he or she is older, it could unlock doors for them. But I'll do whatever you want."

Crystal sighed. "Can I think about it? I'd like to talk to Clint and see what he says. It's not that I'm against it, I just don't want it to create obstacles."

"Of course," David said as he squeezed her hand. "We've got time and I'm sure there will be other things that come up that I'm going to ask you about."

She nodded just as the waiter set down a big plate of fried shrimp.

"Oh, my favorite," she said.

"I remembered you mentioning that," David said.

"How come I didn't know about this," Tyler asked.

"Because you didn't ask," she said, spearing one of the shrimp and putting it in her mouth.

She raised her water glass and the other two men did as well.

"To the baby. May you have the best life ever," she said as they clinked their glasses.

Right now her heart was filled with so much joy and love, she didn't know how she could contain it any longer.

CHAPTER 10

A month later, Crystal thought she was going to die. She didn't just have morning sickness, she was deathly ill with it. And eating didn't help. Her nausea lasted most of the day. About the time for bed, she would feel better.

Between the fatigue and nausea, she was spending most of the day in bed.

For the sake of the baby, she would try to make herself eat, only to throw it back up. She'd become well acquainted with the porcelain god. Bowing down to him all day long, not because she wanted to, but out of necessity.

As much as she wanted this baby, she prayed this would end soon.

She hadn't spoken to Tyler or David in over a week. She'd been too weak.

This morning while she was bent over the toilet, losing everything, she heard a knock at her door.

Lying on the floor, she was too weak to get up and answer it. Whoever it was would have to wait.

Then she heard someone coming in through the front door.

What the hell?

But she was too weak to care.

Lying on the floor, she waited for the would-be robber to find her. But instead Tyler walked into the bathroom.

"Crystal, are you all right?" He rushed to her, kneeling beside her.

No, she wasn't all right. She spent every day throwing up, her stomach sore from the gagging and retching. She just wanted to be left in peace.

"No," she moaned. "Morning sickness."

"The hell it is," he said. "You're ill. I'm calling the doctor."

She'd been thinking about doing that all morning, but she just couldn't summon the energy to get up off the floor and find the phone.

"Do I need to call an ambulance?"

"No, it's just morning sickness," she said. "I'm sure it will pass in a few weeks."

Moaning, she rose to sit up, then another wave of nausea hit her.

"When was the last time you ate?"

"Last night," she said, rising to her knees and then once again tossing her cookies. Tears sprang to her eyes. She wasn't used to being sick. She was an independent woman who could take care of herself.

Tyler pulled her hair back away from her mouth. Why was he being so nice?

When she finished, he handed her a washcloth to wipe her mouth and face. She felt so grimy.

He disappeared into the kitchen and she heard him talking

on the phone. When he returned he'd brought her crackers and water.

"Here," he said. "See if you can get these down. The doctor said you are to come in now. Do I need to help you dress?"

Oh, that was all she needed, him helping her put clothes on.

"No, I can manage," she said, feeling so weak and yet not wanting his help.

Taking her hand, he helped her to her feet. Turning toward him, she saw a square cracker he held out to her.

"That's not helped," she said.

"Just try one. For me," he said.

Raising her brows, she took the cracker from his hand. "And when I throw this up, what then?"

"Then, I'll agree with you that it's not helped," he said.

She took a bite. "I think that will be the first thing we've agreed on."

"You haven't gotten sick yet," he said.

"Oh, just wait. It's coming. Now, I'm going to go get dressed before I spew again," she said.

After walking into her bedroom, she closed the door.

Quickly, she dressed because she feared how soon she would start puking again. She'd managed to get her clothes on before the cracker decided to return. She hurried into the bathroom and knelt over the toilet, then lost the crackers that were supposed to make her feel better.

Tyler came into the bathroom.

"All right, you win. The crackers didn't help," he said.

Closing her eyes, she let the nausea wash over her. How could she do this for nine months?

"I didn't want to win. I wanted to lose," she said, gagging.

"Come on, we need to get you to the doctor. I don't think this is normal," he said.

Feeling like a limp noodle, she let him help her out the front door.

"How did you get into my house?"

For a moment, he was quiet. "Even a lawyer can learn things from his clients. I had a client who taught me how to pick a lock. It was a ploy we used to try to get him off. But instead, he served two years for breaking and entering," he said. "Me, on the other hand, I know how to pick a lock."

That didn't make her feel good. In fact, it was worrying.

"What made you decide to check on me?"

"I've called and left you three messages and David has left you several messages," he said. "We were worried about you. Scared for you."

Even her best friends had not realized that she disappeared off the radar because of this morning sickness that lasted all day. Sickness that wouldn't let her keep any food down and that worried her. The baby needed nourishment.

"Sorry, I haven't looked at messages. I've been hugging the toilet. We've developed a very close relationship."

He opened the door to the SUV and she climbed inside and then he shut the door behind her. When the car began to move, nausea rose in her throat.

"Oh no," she said.

"Here," he said, giving her a plastic bag. "I grabbed a couple of these, just in case."

Thank goodness he'd thought she might get sick, because as much as she didn't want to, she was once again gagging, the need to vomit overwhelming her.

Who knew that pregnancy could be so challenging? But

she wouldn't change things one bit. But it was embarrassing to vomit in front of someone she barely knew.

"There are wet wipes inside the glove compartment," he said.

"Thanks," she said, leaning back against the leather seats.

"Do you regret getting pregnant?"

"No," she said. "Never. This is what I want."

She was certain he knew her background, but she wasn't going to bring it up. She told very few people about her family. For one reason, it was too painful.

They arrived at the doctor's office, and instead of sitting in the waiting room, she was taken back to the nurses' office immediately.

They had her lie on the table and asked her all kinds of questions.

When Dr. Jane came in, she shook her head at her. "Morning sickness. Sounds like yours is more like hyperemesis gravidarum."

"What's that?"

"It's extreme persistent nausea caused by rising levels of HCG and estrogen. You're pregnant," the doctor said.

She took her blood pressure and her vitals and she pushed aside her pants and listened to the heart beat. "Here, listen to this."

The doctor put the stethoscope to her ears.

Stunned, Crystal listened to the heart beat and a rush of love and joy filled her. "Tyler, listen. I can hear the baby's heartbeat."

She put the stethoscope up to his ear, wishing David was with her.

"Did you hear the baby's heartbeat?"

"Yes," he said in awe. "What's making her so sick?"

"Some lucky women get the worst morning sickness there is. I think Crystal is one of those women. I'm going to have the nurse give you an IV. I think you're dehydrated. Then I'm giving you some anti-nausea pills and a pressure point wrist-band that people use for seasickness. We've got to watch this because we don't want you to get dehydrated. And the baby needs you to eat, even though you don't want to."

"I'll throw it up," she said. "All I do is throw up after I eat."

"Hopefully once you start taking these pills, you'll be fine," Dr. Jane said. "But we've got to keep a close eye on you, and if you don't keep any food down in twenty-four hours, get back in here."

While the nurse put the IV in her arm, Dr. Jane patted her on the shoulder and told her she hoped to see her in a couple of weeks at her regular appointment.

Tyler stepped out of the room with the doctor and Crystal feared what he was asking her. And yet she had nothing to hide, she'd done nothing wrong.

When he came back in, he took her hand. "David and I were talking and we think it's a good idea for you to move in with us."

"Us? I didn't think you two lived together?"

"We don't, but when he got ill, I moved in to watch over him," he said.

It seemed strange that the two of them were living together. And now they wanted her to join them. She could work from anywhere, though for the last week, she hadn't done any work at all. In fact, it was a good thing she had the court settlement to live on, but she did enjoy her work.

How sick was David for Tyler to move in and take care of him?

"I really like my own bed better. Besides, I've got to get some work done," she said.

"Look, you would make my life a lot easier if you would move in with David," he said. "That way I can look out for both of you."

Something wasn't adding up and she didn't know what. Maybe they really were gay and they just weren't telling her. It would be all right. She didn't care as long as she wasn't engaged to one of them.

If she did move in with them, maybe she'd find out what their deal was. Maybe she could see for herself what was really going on between the two of them.

"As long as David and you as his lawyer realize I'm not giving this baby up. This baby is mine," she said.

He laughed. "Thank goodness for that. I don't know much about babies and I wouldn't know how to take care of one."

"What about David?" she asked.

A funny expression crossed his face. "You don't have to worry. David knows how much you want this child. All he asks is for permission to see it occasionally. You've got nothing to worry about."

She sighed. After going through this, before labor and delivery, she knew she would fight anyone who thought they were going to take this child from her. Yes, she was worried because David was a freaking billionaire and legal costs were nothing to him.

But he had agreed and she had a signed contract saying she had sole custody of the child. This baby was hers.

The bag of fluid was almost empty, and strangely enough, she felt better. Maybe she had been dehydrated.

The nurse came back in and pulled the needle out of her arm. "All right, you should be feeling better."

"I am," she said.

"That doesn't mean it won't come back," she said as she looked at Tyler. "Don't let her get dehydrated again. That only makes it worse."

"Yes, ma'am," he said as he helped her sit up. "She's going home with me."

She hadn't agreed to go, but yet it seemed like it really was a good idea. Maybe she needed someone to make certain she didn't pass out on the floor again. Already she'd done that once.

Helping her off the table, she glanced at him. "All right, I'll move in with you and David for a few days, but I need to stop and get my things."

"No, you need to rest," he said. "I'll take you to David's and get you settled. Then I'll go back and get your things."

And how would he know what she needed? As if he read her mind, he smiled at her.

"Make me a list," he said.

As they walked out of the doctor's office, she turned on him. "You have no idea where I keep my personal things. How are you going to pack a suitcase for me?"

A grin spread across his face. "You're right, but I've gotten into women's drawers before. I can find whatever you need."

"And if you don't find everything?"

"Then we'll place an order and get what you're missing," he said. "I don't know why we didn't think of this before. This way we'll make certain you're doing well and you're getting the right foods. David has a wonderful cook."

He had a cook? She wouldn't have to worry about cooking for herself and the baby? No, it wasn't a reason to move in with him for the entire pregnancy, but maybe for just a few days or until she felt more like herself, she could be pampered.

Thirty minutes later, Tyler pulled up in front of a sprawling mansion on the beach. She glanced at him, stunned with disbelief. A sense of awe filled her and also trepidation.

"I knew he was rich. What the hell did he do to make this kind of money," she said staring.

"Only the most popular video game in the history of gaming. Now do you understand why I worry that someone is going to take advantage of him?"

"Yes, but it won't be me. The man has given me my dream. I would never do anything to harm him."

CHAPTER 11

*T*yler had never been so afraid as when he walked in and found Crystal on the floor. He'd been terrified she was seriously injured or hurt or having a miscarriage. And God knew he didn't want her to have a miscarriage.

This child was one of David's last wishes, and while he hoped and prayed for a miracle concerning his boss and friend, the chemotherapy was killing him. He was losing weight and sick all the time. Tyler had finally moved in to make certain someone was looking after him.

It was the least he could do when his friend needed him. And now it seemed like he would be taking care of both David and Crystal. He just hoped and prayed that she wouldn't lose the baby.

But seeing her this morning had nearly knocked the breath from him. As much as he didn't like the fact that she was having David's child, he understood her reasoning. And after seeing what was happening with her, he admired her courage.

They walked into the house from the garage and she seemed to be amazed by the house. "Wow, this is fancy."

"You're going to be in the guest room upstairs," he said. "I'll show you to your room."

"Where's David?" she asked. "I want to tell him we heard the heart beat at the doctor's office."

That had been amazing, even astounding if he wanted a baby. The *thump thump thump* of the little peanut had filled him with hope.

"He's in his room resting," he said. "You'll see him at dinner tonight if you feel like eating."

With a sigh, he led Crystal up the stairs to the guest room. He was staying in the room two doors down and David was on the main floor. His balcony doors led out onto the private beach.

"Is there something wrong with him? Something I should know about?"

Tyler wanted to be honest with her, but that wasn't his call.

"Not that I know about," he lied, but he didn't know how to tell her the truth without disclosing David's confidentiality. It was David's place to tell her, not his. And he would protect David's secret as long as he wanted him to.

He opened the door to her bedroom and she glanced in. Big patio doors looked out onto a balcony and the ocean.

"Oh my," she said. "This is beautiful."

"Yes, it is," Tyler said, joining her at the windows as they gazed out. "There's a private beach right out the doors and you're welcome to go swimming anytime."

With a sigh, she turned away from the view. "A woman puking on the beach is not exactly inviting."

He gave a chuckle as he reached out and touched her arm. "Maybe that will soon be behind you. The bathroom is through that door. Please don't let me find you lying on the floor dying again. You scared me this morning."

Turning to him, she chuckled. "Think of how I was feeling. Frankly, I was wishing I was dead when you found me."

Never before had he been so afraid. So scared that she had miscarried.

"I was afraid you were," he said. All he could think about was how David was going to be so upset. Thank goodness, she was all right. Thank goodness, she was still the same smartass.

"I'm sure that would have made you happy."

"No, you're wrong. David wants this child so badly, and I want him to be happy."

Nine months was a long time for a dying man and he wanted him to hold his child before he died, if he had to go. Tyler still prayed for a miracle.

Gazing at her, he knew what she was thinking and chuckled. If only she knew that the two of them were just friends.

"You now suspect all men of being gay, don't you?"

"If the shoe fits," she said. "I'm not against someone being gay as long as I'm not supposed to marry them."

"He's my friend. He's my boss, and no we are not gay."

She gave a little laugh. "You're getting very good at reading my mind."

"With your past, it's not too hard. I owe David a lot."

Turning to him, she tilted her face up and a tingle of awareness shimmered down his spine.

Even though she'd been throwing up, she was still so very beautiful, and now that she was with child, she appeared delicate. Her face was flawless and she had an ethereal beauty about her.

A beauty that seemed to reach inside his chest and he couldn't help but wonder how she would taste. How it would feel for his fingers to slide down her arms, touching her silky skin.

Staring at her lips, he wanted to kiss her, but that was probably not a good idea.

"I think I'm going to rest," she said. "I'm feeling really tired. Here is my list of items and my key. Don't break in again."

A grin spread across his face.

"Dinner is going to be at six thirty. Rest until then. I'll be back with your suitcase filled with things you need, including your laptop."

"And no snooping around," she said. "Not that I'm hiding anything, but it's none of your business."

A chuckle came from him. "Where do you hide your porn?"

"What?"

"Oh come on, you must have some porn somewhere," he said, teasing her.

"I hate to disappoint you, but there is no porn in my house," she said. "But good luck searching for it and I better not find any when I get home, because then I'll know you planted it."

A grin spread across his face. It was so tempting to do something off the wall so she would know it was from him, but he couldn't do that to her.

"Are you feeling any better?"

"Yes," she said. "I think the pills the doctor gave me are helping."

"Good," he said. "Rest. I'll be back soon."

Sitting on the bed, she kicked off her shoes and lay back on top of the comforter. Just gazing at her, it was all he could do not to join her.

But he had things to do. Now he would be taking care of two people.

CHAPTER 12

*D*avid had never felt so sick in all his life. And he still had another five treatments to go. How in the world could he survive these, and he wondered if they were even working.

He got out of bed and went outside to the deck. It was the first time in days that he'd ventured out. About the time he started to recover, it would be time for another treatment and the doctor warned him they would get worse.

Reclining in a lounge chair, he glanced out at the ocean and watched as Crystal strolled along the beach. She was alone and he wondered where Tyler was.

When she saw him, she waved and came toward him.

"Hi," she said.

"Hello," he said. "Have a seat."

She dropped into a beach chair and he thought she'd never looked more beautiful.

This morning, he'd been too sick when Tyler told him he was going to check on her.

Her face was pale.

"Are you feeling all right?"

"I'm better. When the morning sickness became this bad, the doctor gave me some pills to take. At least until this stops."

Sitting back, she gazed out at the ocean. "This is so calming. Listening to the waves slide against the shore, the wind blowing, and just sitting here relaxing."

"Yes," David said. "It's my favorite place."

"I can understand why."

They sat there staring at the ocean and enjoying the breeze.

"Oh, today when Tyler took me to the doctor, we heard the baby's heartbeat."

He wanted to go with her. But he'd spent the day in bed when he wasn't hanging his head over a bucket throwing up. It hit him in waves. He'd be fine and then suddenly he would lose everything.

"How I wish I had been there."

"Next time," she said. "You need to hear the heartbeat. It made this pregnancy seem so real."

He reached over and took her hand. "I'm so excited about this baby."

"I know, me too," she said.

With her living here, there was no way he could keep his sickness a secret from her and yet she needed to live here so Tyler could keep an eye on both of them. So that his cook could make certain she ate well. So that he could watch his child grow.

But there was no way he could keep his illness a secret from her.

Squeezing her hand, he gazed at her. "I need to tell you something."

"Are you going to tell me what's wrong with you?"

The woman was no dummy. Even she noticed he was not well. All he had to do was look in the mirror and see the dark circles beneath his eyes and the way his skin looked sickly.

"Yes," he said. "I can't hide my illness any longer."

Tears welled in her eyes. "It's serious?"

He chuckled. "Very. I have pancreatic cancer."

She gasped her hand covering her mouth and she gave a little sob.

"No," she cried. "Is this why you wanted to have a child."

"Remember how I said you wouldn't have to worry about me interfering?"

"Yes," she said.

"I'm hoping and praying for a cure, but I fear I may only gain enough time to see the baby born. Believe me, if I could, I would be here to watch my child grow, but I don't know if that's going to be possible."

For a moment, she didn't say anything but rather gazed out at the ocean, watching the ebb and flow of the waves.

He felt the need to assure her.

"I knew I was ill when we first talked, but even then, I didn't think I was dying. Now I'm no longer certain. I wanted a child, a part of me to be left behind on this earth. Sadly, I waited too long before I thought about finding a wife and creating a family."

A tear trickled down her cheek and she wiped it away.

"Does Tyler know?"

"Yes, but he's having a hard time accepting that this is the end for me," he said with a sigh. "He keeps telling me we can beat this. Believe me, there is nothing more I would like than to watch my child grow to be an adult."

They sat in silence with her holding his hand. She was crying and he didn't want her to be sad. He'd led a good life. He'd accomplished so much, and now she was giving him what he wanted. A child. Someone he could leave everything to. And yet he knew she probably didn't realize that he wanted this baby to inherit his company, his billions, everything.

That would come with time. But for now, he just wanted to comfort her. He didn't want her upset and crying.

"I wish you would have told me this before I became pregnant," she said.

"Would it have made a difference?"

She sat there and then slowly she shook her head. "No, but now this child will never have a chance to get to know you."

It was true and it was one of the things he worried about.

"Once I read about a woman who was dying and she didn't want her small daughter to forget her. So she made a series of videos for her to watch. One for every birthday and then also several on just things she wanted her daughter to know. Things like how to apply makeup, dating and relationships, and the importance of going to college. If she couldn't be there to help her daughter, then at least she could still help guide her this way."

Gazing out at the ocean, David thought about what he would want to tell his child. There was so much he could say to him. Tell him about his family history, the business he'd created, and how he met his mother. How he'd made the mistake of letting his work control his life until it was too late. There were so many things he wanted to impart to him, even if he couldn't be here in person to do it.

"That's a wonderful idea. I'll set up a video room in one of the guest rooms. Even if I'm not here, at least my child will hear from their father."

They sat in comfortable stillness for the longest, listening to the waves crash against the shore.

"I'm not pressuring you, but I hope that you will move in with me and Tyler. This way, he can watch over both of us and I can watch your belly expanding with my child."

Her eyes stayed on the ocean.

"Tyler hates me. Are you certain we won't make your life miserable?"

He chuckled. What he saw was she and Tyler hadn't recognized yet that they were attracted to one another and were both fighting their attraction. Especially after they had met on that silly cruise.

"No, I don't believe that," he said.

"He was sweet to take me to the doctor today, but remember, he thinks I'm that crazy woman he met on the cruise. And I was kind of nuts after having my third engagement end. But you know, if I hadn't ended that engagement, I would never have met you. And I wouldn't be expecting a child, and right now, I feel content. The only thing that would be better is if you were healthy."

Squeezing her hand, he sighed. "If I were healthy, I would not have made the decision to slow down working or to have a child."

She nodded and he saw the tears building again.

"If I stay here, how can I set up a nursery?"

There was a simple solution to that and he oddly wanted to be a part of this process.

"Why not create a nursery here in the house," he said. "We

could take one of the guest rooms and turn it into a baby room."

She frowned at him. "But I'm not going to stay here forever."

If he had his way, she would. But that was for a later conversation. Right now, he just wanted to get her to live with him.

"You could create it here at the house and then when you moved out, I'll hire a moving company to take everything to your home. I'll even hire a painter if you wanted to paint the nursery."

A smile crossed her face as she leaned back and closed her eyes. "It would be such a hardship to live here. The ocean, a maid, a cook."

"I've already told Maria to make certain our meals are healthy so you get plenty of good nutrition for the baby."

She laughed. "So that you can hear me throwing up at all hours of the day?"

He grinned. "I'll join you. My next round of chemo is next week, and I'll be down starting about two days after it for several weeks. About the time you start to feel better, they zap you again. I'm so sick of it, and I'm not even halfway through the treatment plan."

They heard footsteps on the stairs and Tyler came in.

"No wonder the house is silent. Both of you are out here," he said.

A gasp came from him and he gazed at David. "You told her," he said. "Or you made her cry."

"Yes, I told her. She knows everything now," he said.

Well, everything Tyler knew. What neither of them had learned was that he planned on having his will redone. Tyler had created it, but there were some changes he needed to make.

Tyler took a lounge chair on the other side of Crystal.

"Are you feeling better?"

"Yes," she said. "Amazing what a little fluid and an anti-nausea pill will do for you."

"Did you tell David we heard the heartbeat?"

"Yes," she said, smiling. "In two weeks, we'll have the first sonogram. This one is intra -vaginal and will only tell us the due date. I would love for you to be there, but not necessarily in the room with me."

Staring out at the ocean, he sighed. He had everything a man could want, but the one thing he desired. To be able to go back in time and find the love of his life and marry her and have children. If he could live his life over, work would not have been as important. Relationships would play a much bigger role.

No matter how much time he had left, he was going to make his relationships with these people the most important thing in his life. And if possible, he was going to live long enough to see this child born.

"I'm starving," Crystal said. "Anyone else hungry?"

"Me," Tyler said. "What about you, David?"

No, he wasn't hungry for food. He was hungry for spending time, however much he had left, with these two.

They brought him joy. They were now his family.

With a sigh, he knew they were waiting for him to answer and even though food was a nauseous subject, he would eat with them to try to rebuild his strength.

"Of course," he said. "Maybe afterward, we could watch a movie together."

Tyler was already standing. David watched as Tyler reached out a hand and helped Crystal to her feet. This was what he wanted. As much as these two didn't realize it, they were perfect for one another.

And it was his hope and prayer that somewhere during these months they were all living together, they would wake up to the fact that they balanced one another. It would be such an ideal situation if his best friend, Tyler, could be the father to his child.

CHAPTER 13

A month later, Tyler walked into the kitchen and found Crystal up on a stool reaching for the crackers.

"What the hell are you doing?"

"I'm getting more crackers for in the morning," she said.

The woman was freaking crazy. How had David thought she would be the person to have his child, Tyler didn't know. But Crystal was senseless.

"Get down," he said.

She turned, her brows rising, her sapphire eyes gazing at him like he'd lost his mind.

"No, I can reach them," she said. "I'm not helpless. I'm pregnant."

"Get down before you fall and lose the baby," he said. "How would you feel then?"

A frown appeared between her brows. "I'm not that far along."

"You're far enough," he said.

He walked over to her and placed his arms on either side

of the stool to catch her if she fell. "Tomorrow, I'm going to tell Maria to hide the stool."

"I feel fine. The nausea medicine works great as long as I take it before I get up in the morning and eat a few crackers."

Already he could see she was starting to show, and while it hadn't been long, there was no way he could let her take a chance on losing this baby. This child, he truly believed, was what kept David alive. Kept him going. The thought of seeing the baby had him doing everything the doctors said and fighting to stay alive. If she lost the child, they would soon lose David.

And Tyler would protect them both as much as he could.

"I'm glad you're feeling better. Now, come down off the ladder," he said calmly.

"Do you ever get frustrated or show any kind of emotion about anything?" she asked.

What was she talking about? He'd been so focused on taking care of David that he had hidden his emotions lately, because if he stopped, he feared he would break down. Losing his best friend would be devastating. Watching him go through chemo was tearing him up inside.

And insomnia was once again his second best friend.

"All the time," he said as she stepped down.

They were mere inches apart, but at least her feet were once again planted firmly on the ground.

"Wonderful," she said. "If we're going to help David, we have to stay upbeat and happy and act like we expect him to be here in nine months. I've been reading up on the psychology of people dying and it's important that we make statements that he will be here next year. At least until we know that the treatments are not working and then we have to accept his death. But, right now, I'm not ready to do that."

It made sense. Tyler was dealing with his own raw emotions. But he told himself he had to focus on taking care of David and now Crystal.

"I don't want to lose my friend."

"I don't want to lose the father of my child."

They stared at one another like they had a common goal and Tyler wasn't sure he wanted to share it with her or anyone else.

"How long have you known him?" she asked.

He sighed. "He was my first big client. Probably not long after I received my law degree. We quickly became friends and then our friendship grew," he said, turning and glancing away. "I can't think of life without him."

She reached out and took his hand in hers, giving him a gentle squeeze.

"I have some close friends like that and I can't imagine losing one of them. But there's hope," she said. "Though the chemo is tough."

"His next treatment is tomorrow," Tyler said.

"Tonight, let's have a party. I'll ask Maria to fix us a great dinner and then we'll do something fun," she said. "Something that will take his mind off of what he's going to experience tomorrow. What does he like to do that is fun?"

David walked into the kitchen. "What are you two doing?"

Tyler frowned. "I caught her crawling up on the stool to get more crackers. But don't worry, she'll not be doing it again."

"I'm okay," she said, smiling at David. "I'm feeling so much better. In fact, we're planning a fun evening tonight."

SYLVIA MCDANIEL

"No more climbing," David said.

"All right," she replied. "What do you want to do tonight?"

A grin spread across his face. "Let's play strip poker."

"Seriously?" Crystal said. "We need a fourth. I'll call my friend Nicole."

Tyler frowned. "Will she play strip poker?"

"I won't play strip poker," Crystal said. "And no, she's one of you lawyer types. Kind of stuffy, overbearing, and egotistical."

Staring at her, he shook his head. The woman was nuts.

"I resemble that remark, but I'm not overbearing and egotistical," he said.

She rolled her eyes. "It's amazing how professional people - lawyers don't recognize themselves. You would think with all their training, they would know their personalities."

Just then she gasped, her hand going to her stomach.

"What's wrong?" David asked, going to her.

"I'm not certain," she said. "It wasn't painful. It felt like a bubble or a pulsing sensation."

David grinned. "I've been reading a book about pregnancy. Sounds like you felt the baby move."

Standing there, she gazed at him. "But it's too early."

"Oh no, it comes around sixteen to twenty weeks. We're at week eighteen."

It was hard to believe she was eighteen weeks pregnant. There was a glow about her complexion and she seemed much more settled and happier. In some ways, Tyler was almost jealous of the way she and David acted around one another.

Even David's demeanor was like he felt better and Tyler could see that this pregnancy was good for him as well.

"You mean I've been living with you guys for a little over a month," Crystal said. "I feel the need to go out and get drunk."

The two men glanced at one another. Tyler remembered the last time she had too much champagne to drink.

She laughed. "It does me so good to see you guys gaze at each other like *oh no, she's going off the deep end. How do we stop her?* The last time I got drunk was on the cruise. The time before that was in college. Though I did get a little tipsy when my friend Jennifer came home to the island."

Her eyes sparkled with tears. "Now she's happily married."

With a sigh, she walked out the door. Tyler felt the urge to grab her and pull her back into the room, but he didn't. Sometimes he just wanted to touch her. To let his fingers trail down her cheeks. To feel her smooth skin beneath his fingers.

And her lips. Dear God, if he didn't stop staring at that full luscious mouth of hers, he was going to die. If only he could taste her one time. Let his tongue roam over her full bottom lip until he was satisfied.

"Call Nicole," David said. "Maybe we can play something fun like Twister."

"Ha-ha," Crystal said. "Even now, my body is not going to twist in weird shapes."

Later that evening, the four of them sat around the table.

"What are we playing?" Nicole asked.

"Yes, we're playing strip poker, but the guys have to play nude. You and I will keep our clothes on."

She glanced at Crystal with a shocked expression on her face.

David chuckled. "Do you see what I have to live with, Nicole?"

"You?" Crystal said, laughing. "Every day, I get up, I exercise, do some work and then I go outside and walk the beach. It's so peaceful."

Nicole smiled. "You seem happy. You deserve to be happy, and living here can't be all bad."

Tyler watched as Crystal's eyes softened and a smile graced her face.

"David has been so kind to open his home to me. I feel better than I did those first few weeks. Life is good," she said.

Life was good except for David's illness. Crystal kept them entertained with her funny antics and her unexpected thoughts.

David smiled. "She's pregnant, how could I turn her away? For a while, she was sick the whole day."

"No wonder we didn't hear from you," Nicole said. "We were starting to get worried."

"How are the other girls? I need to call them. Maybe we should have a girls' night out here. If David approves," she said.

"Of course," he said. "I'd rather you were here than out at a bar or restaurant and Maria could fix dinner."

"We'll do it then," Crystal said. "I'll call the other girls on Monday."

Tyler shook his head. He'd never met her friends, but already he could just imagine they were going to be as interesting as she was. Especially after she'd told him about Jennifer and now he'd met Nicole. The only one he'd yet to meet was Amanda.

"I gotta go pee," she said suddenly standing and going upstairs.

"There's a bathroom right down here," David said.

"Sorry, but men use that bathroom. I like my own," she said, hurrying up the stairs.

Tyler shook his head, remembering his sister's first pregnancy. "Just wait until she's nine months and the bathroom is upstairs. She'll change."

Nicole, a beautiful auburn-haired woman with emerald eyes, gazed at the two men. As a lawyer who worked in the district attorney's office, she was a quiet woman, and Tyler could see she was intelligent and very people-savvy. "She's happier than I've seen her since the accident. After the botched wedding, we were all so worried about her. I think this pregnancy and you guys are good for her."

David looked confused. "What accident?"

Tyler knew but had never divulged the information to him. Some things were better kept private. It was her choice whether or not to tell them, but it had come up in the background check.

After he'd read the full report, he understood her need to have a family of her own.

"What happened with the first engagement," David asked.

Nicole gave him a frown. "You should ask her that question."

"I haven't wanted to bring it up," he said. "I keep hoping she'll tell me."

"Let's just say it wasn't long after the accident. She'll have to tell you the rest," she said.

Just then Crystal came running back down the stairs. "Let's play before my bladder goes off again."

"What if we play Mexican Train?" Nicole asked. "That way I stay out of trouble with my boss – the district attorney. I would hate to go to jail because of playing poker with you guys. But then again, you'd be right there with me."

Tyler glanced at David. He could see that he was already getting tired and wouldn't last long.

"Of course," Crystal said. "Me and David against you and Tyler."

They fist-bumped and Tyler wanted to beat her so badly at dominoes. He shouldn't feel that way. He shouldn't, but if he couldn't kiss her, then he wanted at least to beat her.

"It's on like Donkey Kong," he said. "Let the battle begin."

A grin spread across her face and she poured the dominoes on the game table. "No cheating, Tyler."

"Let's make this interesting. The team that loses buys the other team dinner at the Lobster Grill."

"Agreed," she replied, "Or you could make us dinner. How is your cooking, Tyler? I know Nicole's is excellent. She was going to become a chef but instead became a lawyer. Are all lawyers good cooks?"

"Hardly. Unless you want grilled steak and then I'm not bad. How about instead, the loser has to read me a bedtime story at night for one week?"

Crystal shook her head. "Now who is going to read Nicole a bedtime story at night?"

"That's all right, I don't want one," she said. "I fall asleep reading case files. Most of them are boring enough. And David would not want to come to my house and read to me."

Sadly, David would not be able. His next chemo treatment was tomorrow and the reason they were playing games tonight.

"I like the restaurant idea," David said. "That, I could at least participate in."

"Then that's what we'll do," Crystal said, giving Tyler a pointed look.

Why did he always feel like she could almost read his mind? Why did it always feel like they could communicate just by staring at one another?

At the end of the night, Tyler was a frustrated man. Not only had Crystal won, but she'd laughed and played so strategically that all he wanted to do was grab and kiss her.

But that was not possible.

David had given him a look that clearly said *you poor fool. I feel for you.*

Damn, they still had five months before she was due. Five months before this baby arrived and Crystal and the infant left the house.

Strangely, he didn't want this time to end. He liked her being in his life and he couldn't wait to see her belly swell with his friend's baby.

What was wrong with him?

CHAPTER 14

*T*wo weeks later, Crystal couldn't wait for the girls to get there. It was the first time in several months that they could all get together.

As they arrived, she met them at the door, giving them hugs.

Jennifer arrived first, and Crystal could see the joy on her face. The woman had gone through a lot to find her happiness.

She gave her a hug. "How's Dylan, that handsome husband of yours?"

"He's great. I haven't seen you since before your wedding. I'm so glad you didn't marry that jerk."

"Me too," Crystal said, happier than ever.

"And look at you, pregnancy looks great on you," she said. "Do you know what you're having?"

"Not yet," she said. "When everyone gets here, we'll all catch up."

"Sounds great," she said.

"Just tell Maria what you want to drink."

After that, Amanda arrived, and she couldn't help but notice the woman looked so stressed, and she wondered which one of her children were acting up. There were big dark circles beneath her eyes and she was pale. Always thin, she looked like she'd lost more weight.

She gave her a hug.

"Jennifer is already here. Tell Maria what you want to drink and we'll all catch up at the same time as soon as Nicole gets here."

In fewer than five minutes, Nicole walked through the door and took one look at Crystal. "My goodness, I think you've grown several inches in the last two weeks. That baby is growing."

Crystal ran her hand over her stomach. "Yes, I now feel him/her kicking me on a regular basis. I'm so excited, Nicole. I can't wait."

She hugged her friend and then they walked together into the living area with big windows overlooking the beach. It was dark, but the stars shined brightly and you could hear the surf as it pounded the sand.

"You lucky bitch," Jennifer said. "What a view. What a house."

Crystal grinned. "When my morning sickness was so bad, they asked me to move in with them. I've been here since then. I'm feeling much better, but I'm enjoying staying with David and Tyler."

Jennifer's brows rose.

For the next hour, they drank wine, except for Crystal who had water, while Maria served them appetizers.

One by one, they went around the room, telling what was going on in their lives.

Jennifer started. "Alex is doing so well in college. I'm so proud of him. Madison graduates from law school next month. She's already accepted a position with a law firm in Houston. And Taylor is going to spend the summer and the next semester in England studying. And Dylan is fantastic. We're happy. Life is good."

Crystal was so thrilled for Jennifer. After being married to a dick, she was finally getting the happiness she deserved.

Nicole sighed. "I was just appointed the biggest murder trial in town. I'm excited and nervous. Other than that, I've not had a date in months. So I'm really bored."

For a moment, Crystal thought about telling her she should date Tyler, but something held her back. She didn't want to share Tyler. She didn't want to share David. They were her men.

Stunned, she thought about Tyler's mischievous grin, and it struck her that after the baby was born, she didn't know if she would see him again and that made her sad. She wanted him in her life and the baby's life. And David...she didn't want him to die.

"What about you, Crystal?" Amanda asked. "How's the pregnancy going?"

A grin spread across her face. "Since I've gotten over the morning sickness, it's been great. Even now, I still get a little nauseous in the morning, but if I eat my crackers, I'm all right. But if I feel bad, I take an anti-nausea pill."

"What are you having?" Amanda asked.

Something was wrong with the woman; she hadn't said much of anything tonight.

"Don't know yet. We did one ultrasound not long after I

learned I was pregnant, but we couldn't see the sex. This next one, we'll find out."

Jennifer hugged her. "I'm so happy for you. I can see how much this pregnancy means to you."

"Yes, I'm happy," she said, thinking there was only one thing that could make it better and that was if David was not sick. But that little bit of information, she would keep to herself. She had not told them that he was the father. Her friends assumed she'd gotten pregnant by artificial insemination, and she had. Only she knew who the father was.

Amanda leaned forward and put her face in her hands.

"I have news," she said and stood, tears streaming down her face. "Eric has decided that he doesn't want to be married any longer. After Garth went off to college, I thought we would soon retire and travel, but Eric had other ideas. Seems he feels like I've been holding him back his entire life. Now he wants to be free and single and date women to do all the things he missed out on when we had to marry."

"No," Jennifer said. "What is it about middle-aged men?"

"Don't know," Amanda said. "The worst was that when the kids came home on spring break. He gathered us all together and told them and me that he was getting a divorce. It was the first I'd heard about him being unhappy. No marriage counseling, just a divorce."

Stunned, Crystal stared at Amanda. How did you live with someone for over twenty years and one day just walk in and say *we're done*?

"Why didn't you call one of us," Crystal said. "We're your friends. You needed us, Amanda."

The woman began to sob. "Because I'm so ashamed. My

husband doesn't want me. After five children, he's decided he wants a younger woman. Someone who won't hold him back."

There was silence in the room and then Jennifer wrapped her arms around Amanda. "We're here for you."

They all went to Amanda and encircled her in a group hug. "You're going to be fine," Nicole said.

"We need to have a bonfire. Time to burn some sage and even some pictures. Anyone have a voodoo doll? Maybe we should stick some pens in Eric," Jennifer said.

Amanda sat surrounded by them. She gave a little giggle. "That would be fun. I've never been single. What do I do? How do I live my life without a husband, and my children... they are devastated. Right now, they hate him."

Jennifer nodded. "Alex hated his father. He caught him cheating on me and his grades plummeted, he was so angry."

"Yes," Amanda said. "My oldest is about to graduate college and he told me to tell his father not to come. How can his father miss his oldest son's graduation? I'm trying to not let them take sides, but it's so hard. I know I made mistakes in my marriage, but I gave it my all."

Crystal didn't know what to say. Divorce had never been in her family. Just an accident that changed everything and left her alone.

"I'm sorry, I wasn't going to tell you guys tonight because we hadn't seen Crystal since her almost wedding and I didn't want to ruin our get-together," she said.

"No," Crystal said, remembering how her friends had rescued her when life had dealt her a huge blow. And how they had warned her not to marry Aaron. "We need each other."

"Yes, we do," Nicole said.

"I would have been hurt if we had learned from someone else and you hadn't told us," Jennifer said.

Picking up a bottle of wine, Crystal refilled her friends' glasses. "To new beginnings. You deserve someone who will love you all your life, not just the early years."

The women clinked their glasses together and Crystal joined in with her water glass.

"So when is the next bonfire," Nicole asked. "I'm ready. And if you need a good lawyer, you can contact me, or what about Tyler? I hear he's very good."

Tyler. His name sent butterflies flitting through her abdomen. It wasn't the baby, no this was the first beginnings of desire. The first feelings she'd ever experienced like this. The first time she wondered what his mouth would feel like against her own.

"Amanda, we're here for you," Jennifer said.

"Thank you," she said. "I just don't know how I'm going to continue on without him. He's always been there."

Crystal felt like the air had just been sucked out of their get-together. What could she do to restore it?

"All right, ladies, tell me something you love about single life. Me? I don't answer to anyone."

"I don't have to cook anyone dinner," Amanda said. "Take out is my friend."

Jennifer laughed. "Well, I'm happily married, but I did enjoy taking charge. Learning I was in control of the bank account and I could do what I wanted with the money."

The sliding glass door opened and Tyler walked in. For a moment, he was shocked to see the women sitting there drinking.

"Ladies, this is Tyler," she said, thinking he looked wind-blown and so damn handsome.

"Hi, Nicole," he said.

"Jennifer," she said, standing up and shaking his hand.

"Amanda," she said, not bothering to stand.

Crystal turned toward him. "Do you do divorces?"

His brows rose and he gazed at her. "You're already getting rid of me?"

The women laughed.

"Yes," she said. "For insubordination."

"Not a reason to get a divorce. We should really try couples counseling," he said, grinning at her.

She shook her head at him. "No, silly, Amanda's husband of over twenty years has decided he wants to try the single life."

Reaching into his pocket, he pulled out his billfold and handed her his card. "Call my office and we'll set up a time to talk. She'll give you a list of things we'll need to talk about."

Shaking her head, she sighed. "I never worried about us splitting up. Never."

Crystal reached out and touched his arm. A tingle of awareness rippled through her. "Thank you."

Grinning at her, he walked on through the room and into the kitchen.

Jennifer smiled and mouthed the words. "He's hot. Is he the father?"

"No," she said, and yes, he was most definitely hot. And it seemed the longer she lived with him and David, the more she noticed him. The more she wanted him.

"When are we holding a baby shower?" Nicole asked.

For a moment, Crystal was speechless. She hadn't thought about her friends giving her a shower.

"Oh, don't act surprised. You know we're going to throw one for you," Jennifer said.

"I'm not due until the end of October."

"And you need to be ready by September. Sometimes babies come early. It's already mid-June. When will you know the sex?"

A grin spread across her face. "This week. We're going for the next ultrasound, and this time it will be done over my belly, so David and Tyler are going to come with me. I'm so excited."

They all grinned at her.

"What I want to know is when are you going to tell us who is the father of this child."

She shrugged. "Not until we're both ready."

That was her and David's and even Tyler's secret.

"You need to have one of those gender reveal parties," Amanda said.

Oh, she would love to, but it all depended on how David was feeling. He and the baby were Tyler and her main concerns.

"Maybe," she said, not ready to commit to anything other than a baby shower.

"Have the hemorrhoids started in yet?" Nicole asked.

She about spewed her water. "What?"

"Oh yes, get ready for ninth-month hemorrhoids."

Jennifer laughed. "Don't spoil the fun for her. That last month is the time when I was ready to do anything to make the baby come. Have sex, jog, castor oil, you name it, I was willing to try it. And, still, each baby took their sweet time arriving."

"Did you have bad stretch marks?" Jennifer asked Amanda.

"I'm using butter on them," Crystal said.

Amanda laughed. "After five children, my stomach looks like a road map." Tears welled in her eyes. "And no man is going to want to see me naked."

"Not true," Jennifer said. "If a man loves you, he won't care about your stretch marks."

Nicole looked at Crystal. "Remind me to never tell these ladies I'm pregnant. I don't think I'll ever have children. Not with these horror stories."

Crystal smiled. "Oh, but you will. Someday, Nicole. Someday."

CHAPTER 15

The three of them traipsed into Dr. Jane's office and the girls behind the desk looked up and smiled. Yes, their circumstances were odd, but she didn't care. Most people probably thought they were one of those couples with more than one spouse, but she wasn't married to either man.

And yet, these last few months, she'd never felt closer to any two people. Even closer than to her best friends.

They were definitely unique. And yet every day, they grew closer and felt more like a family. Every day, she wondered if the baby would look like David or her. And every day, she feared more for his health.

His color was not good, and just when he got over the chemotherapy, it was time to do another round. She didn't know how long he could continue.

Sitting in the waiting room, the other women gazed at them.

"Do you want me to record this today?" Tyler asked.

"Yes," Crystal said.

David smiled but didn't say anything.

The room was filled with pregnant women at varying degrees of pregnancy. Soon she would reach these stages and she couldn't wait. It was hard to believe they were already at almost six months. Two months had passed since Tyler insisted she move in where he could watch over them both.

She had graduated into maternity clothes and the baby kicked on a regular basis.

The morning sickness was now under control, but she had yet to leave and move home. In fact, she didn't want to. She wanted David to watch her belly grow with his child, knowing that this baby would be so loved.

Every day, she waited for Tyler to come home where they would talk about David and how he was feeling. Every day, he would ask her if she was all right. Every day, she enjoyed being with him. And yet, soon, she would go home.

But today, they were here at the doctor's office getting another ultrasound.

The first one had been done right after she learned she was pregnant. It had not shown much at all, but rather verified the due date. It had been done vaginally and she had not allowed the men to follow her into the room. Today would be different.

For the last several days, she'd been looking at cribs and doing research on which one was the best to buy. David and she had spent time gazing at different designs. Tyler just groaned and walked away.

"I'm thinking we should do the nursery in a purple color," she said, looking at different variations of the color.

"What?" Tyler said, indignant. "Pink for a girl and blue for a boy. Don't go all weird on us."

"But I was wanting a gender-neutral color," she said.

"Purple is not that color," Tyler said. "Maybe yellow."

David chuckled. "Let's wait and see what we're having. Then we can choose the color."

"Purple is gay," Tyler said, his voice carrying and several women glanced up and frowned at him.

"No, it's not," Crystal replied, looking at him like he was crazy. "It's a color. It has no gender identification."

David looked at Tyler. "Purple is the color of royalty. And that's about all I know. I would recommend that you wait until we learn what we're having before you start doing a color analysis. And no color is gay."

Crystal glanced at David and shook her head before she turned to Tyler.

"When do you work? I'm shocked that the partners haven't fired you yet."

He grinned. "Whenever I want to work, that's what I do. Why?"

"I was hoping you'd have somewhere you needed to go," she said.

His expression changed to one that appeared appalled, his mouth open, his brows drawn down in a frown.

"And miss out on learning what we're having?"

She needed to dispel any ideas he might have regarding this baby.

"*I'm* having the baby. *David* is having a child, and you didn't want this child," she said. "You tried to talk David out of doing this."

"You're right I did and I was wrong," he said, looking all innocent.

The man should have been an actor.

Amazed, she stared at him. He was admitting to being wrong about her having David's child.

"Well, that's a welcome change," she said.

He shrugged. "I was doing my job, and at the time, you had acted in an indiscreet manner. I mean asking me to unhook your wedding gown and throwing it overboard. That woman was certifiable."

"Wait," she said, gazing at him. "Do you no longer believe I'm crazy?"

He chuckled. "I wouldn't go that far."

The waiting room grew silent and she looked around. Every woman stared at Tyler like they wanted to pounce on him and beat him to a pulp.

David laughed, covering his mouth with his hand.

"You two find the most interesting topics to argue over and in the strangest places. Thank you, Crystal and Tyler," he said as he glanced at Tyler. "You might need security when we leave here. One of these ladies is likely to take you out."

"I'll say," Tyler said, picking up a magazine. "All I wanted to do was warn her about the dangers of choosing a color for the nursery."

"At least you made brownie points admitting you were wrong," she said. "Though the crazy statement kind of erased that."

"It was a weak moment," he said. "Besides, I'm his attorney and I'm supposed to warn him when I think he's about to jump off a cliff. Or at least give him a parachute."

Right now, she enjoyed him feeling a little uneasy. The pregnancy hormones had her feeling intense sexual desire, even for Tyler. Though they often teased one another, there were times she felt the urge to pull his mouth to hers and taste him.

But then she would shake herself and remember he thought she was crazy, and if she kissed him, she would only be confirming his belief. It had to be the hormones.

"Crystal," the nurse called from the doorway.

It was time to get their first glimpse of the tiny one she already loved. Time to see if he or she was growing and healthy and if they were having a boy or a girl.

Taking David's hand, they walked through the door. Tyler hurried after them.

"I'm not missing this," he said. "I'm the godfather. You're not leaving me out."

"Godfather?"

"Don't listen to him, Crystal," David told her.

"We couldn't leave you out, even if we wanted to," she responded.

David laughed and shook his head at them. He was having a good day and she liked hearing him laugh. She loved seeing him smile and that sparkle in his eyes. Today was a good day and she was grateful.

While she wanted to send Tyler out the door, David wanted him there. And she would do whatever she could to make certain David was happy.

Why did she get the feeling that these two men, even though they weren't married, would be here by her side throughout this pregnancy?

"The technician will be right in," the nurse said.

They stood there looking awkwardly at one another and she realized this would be the first time they would see her expanding belly.

"Have a seat, gentlemen. We're about to see our baby," she said, determined not to worry about how she looked. Yes, her skin was stretching to make room for the baby. They could just deal with seeing it.

She took a seat on the edge of the examination table. Excitement filled her as they waited.

"I'm betting it's a girl," Tyler said.

"A boy," she responded. "If it's a boy, you're buying dinner tonight at the fanciest place in town."

David snickered. "I'm going to say a boy, though I will love this child regardless."

Finally the technician walked in.

"Good afternoon," he said and proceeded to ask her questions about her pregnancy. Finally, after he'd gotten all the information he needed, he turned on the machine.

"All right, lie back here and I'm going to raise your shirt and pull down your pants to get to the abdomen so we can take a look at your baby."

Tyler moved his chair so that he could see the monitor better.

"The father is welcome to come around and watch the monitor," the technician said.

David rose and walked around. He took her hand and she squeezed it.

The man squirted lube onto her stomach and then placed the transducer on her extended belly and moved it around.

She stared at the monitor and when the baby came into view, she gasped.

"David, look," she said.

"Do you want to know the sex?"

"Yes, please," she said.

"Look right here. That's not an innie."

"It's a boy," David said, smiling. "A son."

"Yes," Crystal said with a smile. It hadn't mattered to her what sex the baby was, but she felt like David wanted a boy. And she was happy he was going to receive his wish.

She glanced at Tyler watching his friend with a sad expression on his face. Tears filled his eyes. At first, she couldn't look at David because she feared how she would react. But then she felt the pull of his gaze and glanced at him.

"Our baby," he said.

"Yes," she replied.

"Look, his hand is moving," the technician said and they all stared at the monitor.

"Is he all right?" she asked.

"From what I can see, he's doing very well. We'll have the doctor take a look and make certain, but I think you're going to have a healthy baby."

As she gazed at the child she had wanted for so very long, emotion gripped her chest as tears filled her eyes. One look at Tyler had her tearing up. The man had to turn away and wipe his eyes. She wanted to reach out to him, to hold his hand and tell him that no matter what happened with David, they would always have his son.

And yet, she didn't want to lose David.

A quick glance at the monitor and she could see their son's little heart beating in his chest.

"Bye, little one. We'll see you in October," she said. "Grow strong."

"November," Tyler said. "He's not arriving until November."

With all her heart, she wanted him to arrive sooner. As

soon as it was safe for him to get here, so he could spend time with his father before he died.

As much as she wanted to believe the chemotherapy was working, she'd done some research and discovered the odds were against David.

The technician took several photos and then turned the machine off.

He handed David the photos. "Here's your son's first pictures."

Again, she looked at Tyler and he smiled at her and wiped the tears from his eyes. For a long moment, they stared at one another and she felt like she could almost read his mind. There was joy at seeing the baby, but sadness with the realization that David would probably never get to watch his son grow into an adult.

Gazing at him, she nodded and tried her best to send him a telepathic message of *I understand*. Time was moving swiftly, and as much as they wanted the baby to arrive, they didn't want David to leave.

"I think we should go celebrate," David said, gazing down at the photos. "I'm overwhelmed with love for this little one."

He turned to Crystal. "Thank you. My heart is overflowing with love. I never thought this was possible."

She squeezed his hand. "Me too, David, me too. I'm so happy."

The technician wiped the jelly from her abdomen and then she pulled up her pants.

Tyler came to her side and helped her sit up. "Are you all right?"

"I'm fine," she said, smiling.

"You're free to go," the technician said as he finished cleaning up the transducer.

With her sitting up between them, they stared at the photos.

"He's the future," David said. "He's the future of my company."

Crystal reached out and laid her hand on David's arm. "And you need to be here to help him learn the business."

David hung his head. "I wish I could be. Truly, I do, but I think Tyler is going to have to be the one to hold his hand and show him how to run the business."

"I'm praying for a miracle," Crystal said as she leaned her head against his arm.

"Me too," Tyler said.

The three of them moved together and they gave each other a hug.

The technician stood at the door staring at them. "Good luck."

"Thank you," they murmured as they helped Crystal stand and walked to the door.

She held David's hand, and she grabbed Tyler's. Let the women in the waiting room think what they wanted. All she knew was that she had to hold onto both of them.

"I'm starving," she said, trying to lighten the mood. "And Tyler is buying."

David chuckled. "Let's go."

They walked out the door with her in the middle sandwiched between them. She'd never been happier.

They were having a son.

CHAPTER 16

*T*yler liked to walk along the beach alone. Here he could think about David and even Crystal without worrying they would see his emotions. Tears often streamed down his cheeks as he walked the edge of the shoreline.

Watching David slowly shrink was heart-wrenching and he worried he wouldn't even last long enough to see his child born.

But Crystal...

Crystal was like a breath of fresh air and this pregnancy was probably the only thing that David was living for right now. Between the nasty bouts of chemotherapy and then recovering each month, it was hard to watch his friend suffer.

And he was right there at David's side, even holding his head when he vomited and getting him to the bathroom when he was too weak. Making him eat something to get stronger. Pushing him to continue to want to live.

This was the toughest job he'd ever taken on, but he would continue for his friend.

Here on the beach, he could shed his tears for the man

he cared about without them seeing his distress, for his friend. For Crystal and the child she was carrying. Here, he could wish she was carrying his baby. The thought shocked him.

Since she'd moved in, he'd tried to avoid her, but there were times he couldn't, and whenever he saw her, he wanted to pull her to him and layer his mouth over hers. He wanted to kiss her until they were both ripping off each other's clothes and finding solace in each other's arms.

This time on the beach was his time to gather strength for what he would face when he reached the house. Because watching someone he cared about die was harder than anything he'd ever experienced.

Slowly walking back to the house, he saw her sitting out on the deck beneath an umbrella. Running up the stairs, he gazed at her, longing to spend time by her side.

"Evening," he said.

"Evening," she replied.

He sank into a beach chair next to her.

"How is my friend's divorce going?" she asked.

"Good. We're hoping to reach a settlement in the next couple of weeks and then finalize it in a month," he said.

"I really thought that Eric would come crawling back to her," she said.

He'd hoped so for the couple's sake and their family, but it seemed that Eric had found himself a girlfriend. So far, Tyler's associates hadn't found any evidence of cheating during the marriage, but still the man was not letting grass grow under his feet. He'd become quite the Casanova.

"No," he said, unable to say anything else to her. "You should call her."

Amanda needed to be the one to tell her about how her husband was doing a side hustle. Probably more than one.

"I will," she said, glancing out at the moonlit night.

For a few moments, they sat in silence listening to the ocean and enjoying the summer breeze.

"He's going to die, isn't he?" she said, gazing out at the ocean.

"I hope not," Tyler said. "He's my best friend. God, I hope not."

But he feared she was right. Facing his friend's death was going to be gut-wrenching.

The urge to touch her overcame him and he reached out and grabbed her hand. He wanted to hold her and kiss her, and that shocked him. The need to feel her body next to his was overwhelming, but he wasn't certain how she would receive him.

"This last chemo seemed to just drain the strength from him. I'm concerned he's not going to live to see the baby born," she said. "And I want him to see his child."

Squeezing her hand, he sighed. "Somehow we've got to help him hang on."

"Do you think the chemotherapy is even doing any good?" she asked. "It only seems to be making him weaker."

For weeks, he'd been questioning this. "I don't know. Maybe we should talk to him and his doctor and see if he should continue."

"If it's going to save his life, he should continue, but if it's only going to make him sicker, it's time to stop."

Holding her hand, they sat there in the dark, knowing the man they loved was losing his battle. The summer breeze blew just strong enough to keep the mosquitos away.

"How are the videos going?"

"Not good. He hasn't had the strength to do them," Tyler said, thinking it had been such a good idea, knowing that his son would love to see his father.

"I hope he can at least do the ones for his son's birthdays."

"Yes," he said, thinking about this child that would soon be fatherless. Tyler hoped it would help David feel like he was going to be part of his son's life.

"What if he lives?"

"Wonderful. Then he still has messages to give his son," she said. "God, I so want him to live. To be a part of his son's life. How could I have ever thought he would not want to see his child, I don't know, but now I want him to see his son every day. I want him here watching him grow."

"Me too," he said, feeling his throat closing with tears. "Me too."

The surf pounded on the sand below them and he knew she was crying. Hell, he was crying. Tears leaked from his eyes as they faced the truth together.

"Somehow we have to prepare for him dying but pray that our preparation is in vain. That he has so many years left," he said, not knowing how she would take his death if she was still pregnant. Regardless, it would be hard on both of them, but to be expecting his child would make it devastating.

"Yes," she said, sniffling. "I've been doing research on what dying people want. I've not known David nearly as long as you have, but I want to honor him. We need to find out what his last wishes are. But we also need to spend as much time with him as we can. Talk to him or just sit with him. You have memories you can talk with him about. I just want to be there for him."

Tyler had avoided talking to David about his last wishes for months. He truly wanted him to get better, to conquer cancer, and live another twenty years at least. But his gut was telling him he needed to prepare for the worst and hope for the best.

They needed to make decisions regarding his will and his wishes and what he wanted people to know.

"I'm going to institute reading night. Do you know who his favorite author is?"

"John Grisham, David Baldacci, and even Dean Koontz," he said.

"I'll make certain I have some of those on my Kindle and I'll read to him. You're welcome to join us," she said.

"What can we do that will be fun for him?" he asked, knowing he would join them for the reading hour.

They sat in silence with him still holding her hand.

"I know what I can do," she said. "We'll fly kites and blow bubbles. We'll act like kids again."

"Oh, I can help out with that. His company makes online games. We'll have a tournament here at the house. Ten kids and the best one will win some kind of prize. He loves to watch the kids playing his games. He says it gives him ideas on how to make them better. How to create the next one they will enjoy."

But it was doubtful that David would be here to create his next video game.

"What about his family? His friends?"

"Let's throw him a party," Tyler said. "Out on the beach on Fourth of July. We'll have games and fireworks and it will be his chance to tell them good-bye."

She nodded. "Let's do our best to make his last months a

happy time for him."

"Yes," Tyler said.

The sound of the waves was soothing, and Tyler knew he would miss this place. Now, he understood why David loved living here.

Glancing at Crystal in the darkness, he asked, "What are you going to do once he's gone?"

She gave a little laugh. "I'll move back home. I'll go back to work and try to put this magical time out of my mind. This time of joy and sorrow. And every day, I'll tell his son about him. What a great man he was and how he wanted to be here for him but couldn't."

An ache filled his chest. He didn't want her to leave. He wanted to get to know her even more. She was not the woman he'd assumed she was on the boat. She was much deeper and he really liked her.

"Promise me that we'll continue to see each other," he said.

Her head whipped around and she gazed at him. For a long moment, she didn't say anything.

"You don't like me," she said softly.

Surprise filled him. He'd created that impression, but that was not how he felt about her now. Maybe it was time to show her his feelings.

"Oh, hell, woman, you're not crazy; you're blind," he said, standing and walking to the edge of the deck. How he wanted to kiss her, to hold her, to let her know that every day he could see himself growing more attached to her.

He heard her come up behind him. "Why am I blind?"

Whirling around, he grabbed her shoulders and pulled her to him. Maybe it was wrong, maybe she would reject him, but he had to try. "Because for weeks now, I've been wanting to do this."

His mouth descended on hers and covered her lips as her arms slipped up around his neck and she pressed her belly into his waist. The baby kicked him and he wondered what in the hell he was doing kissing a pregnant woman. But he couldn't release her mouth just yet.

This had been building for months, and he couldn't hide his attraction, the passion he felt for her any longer. Yes, on the boat he'd been an idiot, but now he knew her and he wanted more.

Oh, how he desired her, but she was pregnant and they were dealing with so much life and death. Beginnings and endings, and in some ways, renewal.

Being with Crystal and holding her in his arms felt like he'd come home. This was where he belonged.

His tongue swept inside her mouth and she moaned.

"Mr. Tyler. Mr. Tyler," he heard Maria screaming. "Where are you?"

They broke apart and he knew something was wrong.

"Maria, out here," he called, running into the house and racing down the stairs.

"Mr. David is not well," she said, her face distraught as she stood outside his bedroom. "He fell. I found him on the floor of his room."

Tyler's heart just about exploded inside his chest as he ran down the stairs to David's bedroom. Racing inside, he saw him lying unconscious on the floor.

"Maria, call an ambulance," he said as he reached for his wrist and found a pulse.

Thank God, he was still alive, but something was wrong.

Crystal came into the doorway and ran to David's side. She felt his pulse and then she listened to his breathing. "It's shallow. We need to get him to a hospital."

"Maria is calling them now," he said.

Tears streamed down her face. "David, can you hear me?"

No response.

"David, please don't leave us yet. We want you to see your son. I want you to make some videos for him, so he knows you. We want to spend as much time as possible with you. Please fight this. Don't go."

His eyelids fluttered and he gazed up at them. "So tired of feeling this way."

Tyler nodded and so did Crystal.

"I've called an ambulance," Tyler said. "I'll be right there by your side."

David sighed. "I love you two. I don't think I'm going to make it."

"We love you," Crystal told him.

"David, you're my best friend. You know I love you," Tyler said.

The sound of sirens could be heard approaching and Tyler didn't think they could get here fast enough.

"I just want to rest," he said. "So tired."

They glanced at one another, their hearts in their gaze just as the paramedics came rushing into the room.

CHAPTER 17

*A*t midnight, Tyler insisted that Crystal go home. She looked exhausted and the doctor had assured them he was not going to die tonight. His vital signs had improved and they were giving him fluids and even a couple of units of blood.

"I've called you an Uber," Tyler said. "You and the baby need to rest. I'll stay with David. If anything changes, I'll call you."

"I don't think I can sleep," she said, leaning against Tyler. "I'm so worried."

"Just try," he told her. "As soon as they get him settled in a room, I'll be home."

Funny that they were starting to call David's house home.

"All right," she said as she hugged Tyler to her. Tonight he'd been kissing her when Maria sounded the alarm. And she'd enjoyed that brief moment of happiness in his arms.

This time, it felt tense; they were both so afraid.

The baby kicked and she realized she really did need to rest.

"The car just arrived. I'll walk you out," he said.

Outside the sliding front doors was a car waiting for her and it wasn't an Uber. It was a damn limo. She turned to face him. "I could have taken an Uber."

"No, you couldn't," he said. "You're pregnant, it's late, and you and that baby need to be taken care of. Besides, my company has an account with them."

She kissed him on the cheek. "Thank you. See you at home," she said, knowing she would not go to bed, but wait for Tyler to come in. Even if it meant staying up all night.

He opened the door to the limo and helped her into the car and then he hurried back into the hospital.

Tonight, sitting out on the balcony, she had seen him crying about David. Hell, they had both cried about their friend and then he'd kissed her. An odd sense of peace had filled her when she'd been in his arms and she didn't know what to think about those feelings.

The driver had her home in less than thirty minutes and had even made certain she got into the house before he drove off. It felt like Tyler had given him instructions that she was to be well taken care of and that filled her with warmth.

She liked him taking care of her.

Inside the house, Maria would be in the servants' quarters asleep, but the big house felt empty, and she couldn't imagine what it would feel like when David was gone.

Knowing she couldn't sleep, she went into the family room, curled up on the couch, and turned on the television. Anything to keep her mind off what was happening at the hospital.

The lights were off except for a light in the hallway that

she'd left on for Tyler. Getting comfortable, she dozed off and soon was sound asleep.

Dreaming, she felt the soft caress of a mouth against her forehead, her cheek, her nose, and even her lips. Opening her eyes, she saw Tyler sitting beside her on the couch.

"Scoot over," he said.

"Hmm," she said, moving as he managed to crawl beneath the throw blanket and was beside her. "How's David."

"He's resting comfortably. He even spoke to me and told me to go home and make certain you were all right. So he knew we were there this evening."

Tyler wrapped his arms around her and pulled her in close. A sense of coming home filled and surprised her. She liked the feel of his muscular body and lying against him.

He kissed the top of her head as she slid her arm around him.

"What are we doing?" she asked.

"We're taking care of our friend," he said.

"No, what's going on between us?" she asked.

"I don't know," he said. "But it feels wonderful."

She couldn't agree more. It felt perfect.

"So am I still blind?"

He laughed. "Yes and no. I've been waiting for weeks to find the right time to kiss you."

She gave a sleepy chuckle. "And I thought you would never do it. I thought you didn't like me and thought I was crazy."

His hand rubbed down her back. "You were. But since I've gotten to know you better, you hide the crazy pretty well."

"So why is a fine upstanding lawyer who likes things black and white doing with a crazy woman who is having his friend's baby?"

Shifting on the couch, he pulled back until he could face her. "Beats the hell out of me. But you do make life interesting."

"I'm not looking for a one-night stand," she said, gazing up at him. "I'm looking for forever. So if you're not, then this thing between us is not going to work."

Maybe this had been her problem with men all along. She wasn't direct enough and didn't ask for what she wanted. If there was going to be another man in her life, he needed to know her needs and her requirements right up front.

"I'm not looking for a one-night stand either. I'm looking for forever, but I will warn you that I'm not one to jump in. After so many divorce litigations, you learn to be careful."

"*Careful*, I'm okay with. Even taking our time, but I'm not sleeping with you until we're married. I'm going to do things the old-fashioned way this time."

A frown spread across his face. "Can we maybe sleep together right here on the couch?"

A smile crossed her face. Right now, that would be perfect.

"My cell phone is here in case the hospital calls. And after today, I would love for you to just hold me. Let me fall asleep in your arms," he said. "I'm hoping it will keep the insomnia away."

She could see the need in his eyes and she squeezed him to her.

"Only if you kiss me again," she said. "That kiss was just starting to get interesting when Maria interrupted."

A grin lit up his face.

"Gladly," he said and pulled her lips down to his.

It was a kiss that had her heart rate spiking. She curled her leg up and over his as he deepened the kiss, his lips commanding her surrender and she gladly gave it up to him. This was what she wanted for tonight.

Finally, a groan escaped him and he pulled his lips from hers. "Damn, that is so good. But if we don't stop, I'm going to be in a really bad situation."

She giggled.

"Goodnight, Tyler," she said.

He pulled her up against his body and she felt like she'd come home.

"Goodnight, Crystal," he said. "Sweet dreams of me."

"Oh no, then *I* might be in a really bad situation."

"Glad it's both of us. Let's just hope that tomorrow is a better day."

"Yes," she said as her eyes once again closed.

But tomorrow wasn't a better day. In fact, it was the worst day and if she'd known what was going to happen, she might have stayed in bed or on the couch.

When she awoke, Tyler was gone. Quickly, she got up, showered, and dressed for the day, wanting to get to the hospital early.

When she came downstairs, Tyler was eating yogurt and he handed one to her.

"I enjoyed sleeping with you," he said. "You purr."

She smiled and then she kissed him on the lips. "You fart in your sleep."

"I do not," he said.

"Well, it wasn't me."

"It must have been the baby," he replied.

"Not yet," she answered. "But I'm sure it's coming."

She took the yogurt he offered her and quickly ate it, but she would soon be hungry again. From the pantry, she grabbed crackers and granola bars to put in her purse. She had learned that if she kept just a little substance in her stomach, she didn't start feeling bad.

"Are you ready to leave?" he asked.

"Yes," she replied and they walked out the door.

Fifteen minutes later, they were in the hospital and Tyler took her hand and led her to David's room.

Before they opened the door, he kissed her on the lips. "Big smiles. We've got to be upbeat and happy for him."

She nodded, though her heart ached.

"David," she said, rushing over to kiss his cheek.

His color was yellow and he looked like he didn't feel good.

"I brought you a book," she said. "Tyler told me you enjoyed this author and I thought you might want to read it while you're in the hospital."

"How are you," Tyler asked. "I had to kick her out of here last night to get her to leave you."

David shook his head and gave a half smile. "I'm glad you did. You need to be concentrating on that baby and not me."

"I'm great at multi-tasking. I can do both," she said, going to his side and taking his hand in hers. "Especially when I'm taking care of two people I love."

A grin spread across his face.

"You scared us so bad last night," she said.

"Didn't feel too great on my end either," he said.

"When is the doctor coming in," Tyler asked.

"The nurse told me he would be in this morning."

Crystal pulled up a chair to his bedside. "Then we're here until he comes in. I even brought snacks, so I wouldn't get sick."

"Please," Tyler said. "That's all I need for both of you to do this at the same time again."

There was silence for a few minutes and then Crystal glanced at Tyler.

"I'm thinking we should have a big blowout for the Fourth of July. Invite your family and friends and cook barbecue and even shoot off a few fireworks. What do you think?"

He glanced between the two of them. "Am I that bad?"

"If you were that bad, I don't think we'd be having a party," Tyler told him.

He grinned. "You might."

Crystal gasped. "No. Don't even say that unless you want to see a pregnant woman cry."

"Let me think about it," he told them. "My family would love nothing more than to see me dying. The vultures will swoop in and be picking my bones."

That didn't sound good.

"Don't they love you?"

"They love my money. The only time I hear from them is when they're going broke. But I would love to see my cousins one last time."

Tyler glanced up at the clock and that made Crystal nervous.

"They don't have to know you're sick," he said. "It could just be a plain old American summer party."

He nodded. "Maybe. Let's see what we learn from the doctor today. They did an MRI early this morning. I'm sure that will tell us what we need to know."

Fear gripped her. They must've been looking to see if the cancer had grown.

A knock sounded at the door and a man in a white coat walked in.

"Hello," he said, glancing at the two of them. "Do you mind waiting outside while I speak to my patient?"

"No," David said, sitting up. "They need to hear this as well as me. These two are taking care of me and called the ambulance."

The doctor nodded. "The chemotherapy is not working and I think it's affecting your quality of life. This type of cancer is very aggressive and it's spreading. We can try another type of chemotherapy, but it will only give you weeks, not years."

Crystal started to cry. She bit her cheek to keep from sobbing, but the tears slowly rolled down her cheeks. Tyler walked up behind her and laid his hand on her shoulder.

"How long do I have," David asked.

"That's hard to say, but I don't think you'll be here at Christmas," he said, his voice sad. "I wish I had better news."

A look of acceptance came over David's face. "As long as I live to see the baby. That's all I want."

The doctor nodded. "At some point, you will need hospice. They will help take care of you. Bathe you, feed you, and keep you comfortable in the end. But you're not ready for them yet."

He nodded.

"Last night in the ER, you were given two pints of blood which should strengthen you for a little while."

David glanced out the window and then turned back to the doctor. "When can I go home?"

"Tomorrow," he said. "I want to run just a few more tests

to make certain I haven't missed anything. Any questions? I'm sorry, David."

They all stared at the doctor as he had delivered the worst possible news.

"No," David said. "Just never planned on going this way."

"No one ever does," the man said. "Call my office if you need anything."

"Thanks," David said.

When the doctor walked out the door, Crystal began to sob and Tyler pulled her into his arms as tears fell from his eyes.

David sat quietly for a moment. "I think we should have that Fourth of July party. One last big blowout before I go."

"Oh no," Tyler said. "We think you should also have a game tournament with the very best players."

He grinned. "That sounds like fun. And a baby shower. I want to see what my son receives."

They nodded. Tyler still had his arm wrapped around Crystal as she cried.

David glanced at the two of them and smiled.

CHAPTER 18

*W*hen David came home from the hospital, he seemed to be feeling better. No more chemo and a week later, he seemed to have more energy and was helping them make plans.

First, he and Tyler set up a gaming convention at a nearby hotel. The proceeds would go to cancer research and the buy-in was consistent with other gaming events. Of course, David donated all the money made from the convention, so he basically paid for the event himself.

Tyler watched his friend talk to all the players and encourage them to finish college and make this their profession. He even gave some of them the card to his Human Resources department, telling them to contact his company about a job.

It was hard for Tyler, knowing this was the last one David would be involved in, and yet David had done so much for this industry. After he died, these kids would look back and know he had helped them.

When the day came to crown the winner, David had a bad

spell, and for a moment, Tyler was certain he wasn't going to make it to the final ceremony, but somehow he found the strength.

The winner won ten thousand dollars and a partial scholarship. Just David's way of encouraging the kids to go to school.

That night as they drove home, Tyler could see the weekend had drained him.

"You need to get some rest tonight," Tyler said.

"Yes, but thank you for helping me with the convention. It was so much fun and I enjoyed every minute."

"I'm glad," Tyler said.

"What's going on between you and Crystal?"

Tyler was almost afraid to tell him and yet his friend should know. "We're just spending some time together being with you."

He didn't want to give David hope that they would fall in love, marry, and live happily ever after. There was no guarantee about that and they could just be growing close because of their love for David.

And yet, this felt special.

"Well, it looks different," David said.

"She's crazy," Tyler said, trying to bring up his old excuses, though he felt completely different about her now.

"You could use some crazy in your life," David said, chuckling. "I highly recommend it."

They rode along in silence for a few more minutes.

"I want to redo my will," David said.

"All right," Tyler said.

"The baby needs a college fund and a trust fund, and there is so much more I want to do. I know you're working on

Crystal's friend's divorce, why don't you have one of your associates come to the house and we can make the changes I want."

Did he really believe that he was going to let someone in his office handle his best friend's will? Especially a man with all kinds of investments, money, properties, and a business.

"No, I'm going to redo your will," he said. "I don't trust anyone else."

David sighed. "All right, but you're making my surprises very hard."

Tyler didn't want anything from David. He'd been his first client, his best client, and his friend.

"I want nothing," Tyler said. "You've given me so much already."

"But I want you to make sure that my son has what he needs. I want you to check in on Crystal. Make certain they're doing all right. I'm tasking you with the biggest and most important thing in my life right now. And he hasn't even been born yet."

Tyler's heart clenched with pain.

"You know I'll do that. You don't even have to ask me."

"And I want you and Crystal to get along. No more fighting," he said.

Oh, if only the man knew. They had taken to walking along the beach at night after David went to bed. It was their time alone together to talk about their dreams, their wishes, and the ordeal they were going through, and then make out like two horny teenagers on the beach.

After the day was over, that was their time. They had not slept together again and she still insisted they were not having sex until they were married. In some ways, that made him appreciate that this time she was not going to get fooled by anyone.

But it sure made for a painfully hard dick at night.

"We're not fighting," he said. "I still call her crazy occasionally. She calls me a narrow-minded lawyer. Then I remind her that I helped her remove her wedding dress on the boat."

The memory had his heart racing. If only he'd sought her out on that boat, but then again, she wasn't ready to dive into another relationship.

"I like Crystal," David said. "She's going to need you when I die. She's kind-hearted and I fear she won't take my passing easy."

"No, she won't," Tyler responded, wondering how his friend thought he was going to take losing his best friend. Even just thinking about it had him tearing up.

He pulled into the driveway and parked his car.

"Have you told Maria?"

"Yes," David said. "I want to make certain she receives a little something when I go."

Tyler leaned his head against the steering wheel. "I hate this."

"I know," David said. "Me too."

"It's not fair," Tyler said.

"No, it's not, but then who said life was fair? Don't wait too long my friend to find love, settle down, and have a family. You never know when it's going to be the end."

Tyler thought of his father and how it had come so quickly for him. No preparation, nothing. Just one day he was here and gone the next. Even Crystal's parents. One day they were here and then they were no longer in her life.

They had both suffered losses and now they would be experiencing a loss together.

"Come on, let's go see how Crystal is doing," Tyler said.

They walked into the house and she had a masseuse waiting on them.

"Gentlemen, meet Sally, she's here to give you both a massage. I thought after your arduous game playing that you might need a little relaxation," she said. "Now I'm going to go in the kitchen to help Maria. We've got a big dinner for you tonight."

Tyler glanced at David. "Are you up to this?"

"Of course," he said and Tyler knew he was lying. But he would do anything to make Crystal happy.

"The massages are only thirty minutes long," she said. "So dinner will be ready in one hour."

The woman motioned them to the table.

David grinned at her. "Oh no, I'm taking my shirt and my pants off."

"Whoops," Crystal said. "I'm leaving."

Tyler wanted her to stay but knew that she wanted to respect their privacy. He wasn't leaving David's side because he feared him getting ill.

Soon, the woman's hands were moving over his muscles. "You're tense."

"Yes," he said. "I am."

"Then I will help you relax," she promised.

Thirty minutes later, David sat up on the table.

"I feel better," he said, smiling.

"Why don't you take my turn," Tyler said, thinking he might never get another massage.

"Are you sure?"

"Yes, I'm going to the kitchen to assist Crystal and Maria."

David lay back down on the table. "Continue."

When Tyler walked into the kitchen, the women were busy making fajitas, David's favorite. They also had a birthday cake with candles.

"Whose birthday?"

"No ones," Crystal said. "But we're going to party like it's someone's birthday."

Maria smiled. "Yes."

Tyler took Crystal's hand. "At first, I thought the massage was going to be too much, but he really enjoyed it, so I let him have mine."

Her hand caressed his face. "I was so afraid that today would be too much for him."

"It just about was," Tyler said.

"How are you?"

"I'm all right. Tired," he said.

"Too tired for a walk on the beach later?"

"Never," he said, looking forward to having time alone with her. Thirty minutes later, Maria carried out the sizzling fajitas and they sat down to dinner.

Tyler noticed that David's face was white, but he didn't say anything. Hopefully as soon as he ate, he would help him get ready for bed.

It wasn't that he was an invalid, but he feared him falling or getting dizzy.

"Whose birthday?"

"Yours," Crystal said. "We're celebrating your birthday once a week. This way, we'll get to celebrate them with you."

Tears burned in David's eyes. "You don't have to do that."

"I know, but I want to," she said. "Besides, I get to eat cake this way."

"Oh, that's the real reason. What do you think Dr. Jane is going to say about that?" Tyler asked.

"She's going to say *you are one lucky woman*," Crystal said, teasing Tyler.

"Thank you," David said. "You treat me so well. I'm so happy that you're both here with me during this time."

An hour later, Crystal met Tyler on the back deck and they walked down the stairs.

"Today was hard," Tyler said.

"I could see it in your eyes," she said.

"He wants me to redo his will," he said. "I don't know if I can."

Crystal took his hand and pulled him against her. "You have to. You're the only one he can trust. And no, I don't want anything. I want the baby to get whatever he wants to give him, but nothing more. He's given me so much already."

"Yes," Tyler said. "He asked me about us today."

"What did you tell him?"

"Not much," he said. "I'm so afraid he'll expect too much."

"Always my conservative lawyer," she said. "Come on. We need some happy time. Let's go swimming in the ocean," she said, running toward the beach.

"It's dark. There are sharks," he replied.

"And there's a naked me waiting for you," she said, laughing as she ran as fast as her pregnant body would go.

"Damn, woman. You're teasing me," he cried.

"No, I'm not, and no, we're not having sex," she said. "But I want to go skinny dipping before I have a baby," she said.

Just then she pulled her maternity top over her head and dropped it in the sand. Next came her shorts and underwear.

"You're crazy," he called.

"And you're a pain in the ass," she retorted as she plunged into the ocean.

Pulling off his clothes, he ran into the ocean after her. Someone had to save her from herself.

CHAPTER 19

*D*avid stood in front of the mirror and gazed at his body. No, it wasn't the body he once had, but he didn't look bad. Hopefully, he wouldn't tire out before the end of the party. And more importantly, he hoped none of his guests realized he was sick.

Against his better judgment, he'd invited his sister, nieces, nephews, and the cousins he grew up with. One aunt and uncle and then his employees. No one knew anything about him being ill and he hoped it would not become an issue today.

Crystal and he had decided not to mention that he was the father of her child. It was better that the family not get involved. Later, he would tell them, but not now.

This week, he and Tyler had worked on the will until Tyler finally told him *that was enough*. There were some things he wanted in the will that he didn't want either Crystal or Tyler to know about.

Tyler told him Crystal had said for him not to give her anything, but how could he not? She was carrying his child.

And from the looks of her expanding waist, his son was going to be a big boy who would hopefully arrive before he departed this world.

In a spare bedroom, Tyler had set up camera equipment and David had been busy making videos for his son. He hadn't expected recordings to be hard, but it was extremely difficult to make the ones for his son's birthdays when he knew he wouldn't be there. And then also to do one about the things you experience in life.

The baby needed a father.

Plus, he wanted them to be upbeat and not sad or depressing. So he only recorded on days he felt good and cheerful.

He'd been going through the photos of his family, and with Crystal's help, was making an album of everyone in the family, so that the baby would know where he came from and what his family looked like.

Since he stopped the chemotherapy, he felt better. Not great. He still grew tired, but at least he wasn't lying in bed wishing he would die while his insides wanted to throw up everything.

All he wanted and prayed for was to see his son born. After that, he had a few other desires, but he wasn't going to put any pressure on Tyler and Crystal. But he could see the way they looked at each other. Sometimes there was enough heat in their gaze to make him jealous.

The guests were arriving and yet he hadn't made an appearance yet. His biggest concern was that someone would realize he was sick and that he would not be on this earth much longer.

It was time to face the people gathered here. The party hadn't started until late afternoon because he couldn't do all day. Plus, for fireworks, they needed the dark. Hopefully, they would all be gone as soon as the fireworks show ended and he could collapse in bed.

Opening the door, he stepped out onto the deck.

His sister was the first person he saw.

"David," she said, hugging him. "How are you?"

"I'm great. Did you bring Jack?"

Her husband was a total dick, but she was married to him.

"He's getting a beer."

"How are the kids," he asked.

"They're out in the ocean already," she said. "You'll see them later."

He'd left her children a small inheritance, not to be received until they attended college. He'd left her a small inheritance, but not much. The only time he saw her was when he invited her over. She never called. She never invited him to visit unless she needed money and then the phone lines heated up.

Tyler came to his side. "The head of Human Resources is here," he said, whispering into his ear. "She wants to speak to you alone."

"Excuse me," he said and made his way to the woman.

When he walked up to her, she frowned and stared at him. "Let's take a stroll along the ocean where we can speak in private."

This sounded ominous.

"There are rumors going around the office that you're getting a sex change."

He busted out laughing so hard, he started crying. "Really?"

"I gather that's not true," she said. "It's just you've been absent for so long that these strange rumors are going around."

Taking her by the arm, he smiled at her. "Thank you. You've made my day today. Yes, I'm sure there are a lot of rumors going around and there will be even more. What I'm going to tell you is in confidence. I'm dying. I have pancreatic cancer and it's not curable."

"Oh no," she said, raising her hand to her mouth. "No."

"It's all right," he said. "I'm leaving the company in very capable hands. It will continue. But I'd like to keep this quiet for as long as possible. I don't want my last days to be filled with reporters waiting outside my door for the news of my death."

With a sigh, she shook her head and closed her eyes. "I'm sorry. You've been the best person I've ever worked for. I'm sorry to hear this."

He nodded. "Thank you. Now let's get back to the party and have some fun. My friends wanted this day to be a happy day for me and I'm going to do my best for them."

The rest of the day went very well. He talked to everyone there. He watched as Tyler and Crystal tried not to touch each other but kept sneaking in little touches here and there. They made his heart warm and he so wanted them to get together.

It would be perfect for his son.

It was a grand day, a wonderful day, and it would be the last time he saw his family.

And yet, they had been standoffish the entire time.

After the fireworks were over, people began to pack up. He stood at the door and told each person that he was so glad they came.

They didn't realize he was saying good-bye forever. After

he died, they would look back on this day and remember how he'd hugged them, knowing it was the end.

As his sister walked up to him, she pulled him aside.

"I need to borrow twenty thousand dollars from you. Jack got fired and we're about to lose the house."

The son of a bitch never could keep a job.

"All right," he said. "Give me the name of your mortgage company and I'll pay them direct."

She frowned and he realized before when they had money problems, he had never done this. He'd just written her a check. But this time, he was going to end their mortgage problems forever.

"I need the money," she said.

Why did it seem like she was lying to him? And yet, he had to help her. She was his sister. And this would be the last time.

"All right. I'll mail you the check," he said. "Tonight is not a good time."

Already he could feel himself tiring and he wanted this party to end. He wanted everyone to go home.

"You can't write me a check now?"

"No, I can't," he said, thinking soon he would collapse. "I'll mail it to you," he said.

"Okay, but put it in the mail tomorrow or I'm going to be in trouble," she said.

Tonight was the first time he heard about her being in trouble.

"Sis, you'll always be in trouble if you stay with Jack. I'll mail the check tomorrow. My one wish for you is that you would leave him. Someday I'm not going to be here," he told her.

Tyler walked up. "Are you all right?"

"Yes," he said. "Sis was just leaving."

He watched as they walked out of the house and out of his life forever. No *thank you*. No remarks of *we're so glad we came*. Nothing but what she needed.

Sometimes having billions only made you a target. And the worst seemed to be family members.

Crystal came up beside him. "You look tired. Did you have a good time?"

He didn't want to disappoint her. She'd been doing so much to make his last days happy. And it wasn't that he didn't have a good time, it was just that dealing with family cast a shadow on the day.

Wouldn't they all be surprised when the bank was gone?

"Yes, I had a good time. Sometimes things never change and my family hasn't changed in years."

She gave him a hug and Tyler took him by the arm. "Let's get you in bed."

"Goodnight," Crystal said and turned away before he could see the tears slipping down her cheeks, but he saw them and knew they were real.

"Goodnight," he said. How many more times would he get a chance to say that to his two closest friends?

CHAPTER 20

*T*he next morning, Tyler slipped a note under Crystal's bedroom door. She saw the piece of paper on the floor and bent down to pick it up. It was becoming harder and harder to do that.

And yesterday, she'd noticed that her feet were swollen last night after the party. She'd been on her feet most of the day, and it seemed that her body was telling her that was a no-no.

Glancing down at her rounded belly, her heart warmed. She loved this baby so much and knew that it would face challenges, but she would always be there for him.

Opening the folded note, she grinned.

The note said: *I'd like to take you out on a date today. How about us driving into Corpus Christi and going to that big name baby store, a movie, and then dinner? If you want to go, meet me downstairs at eleven.*

Her heart warmed. While they had been fooling around, kissing, laughing, and having fun together in the evenings, they had not been on a date.

This felt special. Maria would be here with David and it would be good for them to take a break.

It was ten thirty and she wanted to look her absolute best. Hurriedly, she put on makeup, chose her prettiest maternity dress, and put on summer sandals.

Funny that she was dating while she was seven months pregnant.

She walked down the stairs and into the living area searching for Tyler. He was talking to David.

"Wow, you look really nice," David said.

"Thank you," she replied. They had agreed not to tell David what was happening between them just in case it didn't work out. She didn't want to get his hopes up and then dash them.

"Are you ready?"

"Yes," she said.

David grinned at them. "Have fun, you two."

His expression was suspicious, but she didn't want to acknowledge that they were a couple yet. She'd been burned three times and this time she was being cautious.

Plus, he looked tired. It would be good for him to rest today.

"Come on," Tyler said. "Let's go baby shopping."

She grinned. "That will be fun."

As soon as they were out of the house, he took her hand and led her to his car, a BMW 8 which was a fast, luxurious car.

"Fancy," she said.

"Yes, I brought out the sports car for you today," he said, grinning. "I get tired of driving that monster SUV I use with clients."

"After you made fun of my Mustang, I'm shocked to see you have a fast car," she said.

"Even lawyers like fast cars," he said. Settling in, they backed out of the driveway.

"Okay, a few rules for today," he said. "Today is about the two of us enjoying one another's company. We're not going to talk about David. We're going to have fun today."

That seemed fair. After yesterday and David's family, she needed a break. The children had been brats who didn't even talk to their uncle. His sister was going to be in for the shock of her life when her brother died, and she felt sad for her.

"Agreed," she said. "Let's have fun."

He sped off and she had to grab onto the door handle.

"But let's not kill ourselves in your car," she said.

A grin spread across his face.

"So are you feeling all right?" he asked.

"After those first few months, I've felt great. Last night, I noticed my feet were the size of an elephant's. I'm sure it was from being outside in the heat and being on my feet most of the day."

He nodded. "The movie theater has those reclining chairs where you can put your legs up."

She smiled. "What movie are we seeing?"

"I was going to let you pick," he said.

"Thank you."

They crossed the large bridge that connected the island to Corpus Christi proper.

"After the baby store, can we go to the mall? Our first date and we're going shopping."

He grinned. "I thought about taking you to the horse races or the dog races or even a play, but I thought you would enjoy going to the baby store more than anything. What is it you need at the mall?"

"I haven't been inside a real mall in forever. I'd like to see what they have in baby things."

"Well, there is a movie theater there," he said.

Brow raised, she turned and stared at him. "Why are you being so nice to me?"

"Crystal, you deserve for someone to be nice to you."

"I know, but they have been incredibly hard to find."

"Maybe you've been looking in the wrong place," he said.

She laughed. "Oh, so I should have had some stranger remove my wedding dress on a cruise before?"

He grinned at her. "I thought you were crazy that night."

"I kind of was. After everything that happened that day. Wow, that was a different life."

He parked the car and came around to her door.

When he helped her out of the car, he leaned and gave her a quick kiss on the lips.

"I've been wanting to do that since we got in the car," he said.

"Hmm," she said. "Why didn't you kiss me on the cruise line? We could have recognized the passion between us right away."

"Because you weren't ready for another man to make a move on you," he said. "But I did think about it. Especially with you sitting there in your underwear."

She laughed. "It was dark and if you'd tried anything, that champagne bottle would have landed on your head."

"Just as I thought," he said. "Come on, let's go baby shopping."

Warmth filled her and she would never have thought she would end up with this man.

When they entered the store, she was amazed. "Oh my goodness."

Tyler laughed at her. "A true woman who is pregnant with a shopping gene."

"Hey, leave my genes alone," she said.

A woman who had just walked in the door looked at her and laughed. "It's a little late for that, honey."

Knowing their situation, she busted out laughing.

Tyler grabbed a cart and the lady behind the counter gave her a clipboard. "Mark down what you like, and then before you leave, register with us so people will know what you want at your shower."

"Thank you," Crystal said almost doing a dance. She was so excited.

"Please tell me you're not sticking to purple," he said.

"No, I'm doing orange," she replied.

"What?" he asked, incredulous.

Laughing, she shook her head. "You're so gullible. I know just how to get you riled."

"And you enjoy doing it," he said.

It was true that they teased one another mercilessly and she enjoyed it. At first, they had been digging at one another, but now, it had switched into more of a fun banter that kept them laughing. And that's what she wanted to do today.

Laugh.

"Have you found the bed yet?"

"No, because I don't want to have to move it after..."

"I don't think you and that baby are going anywhere until he's gone. I'll help you move it."

"Even if you hate me again?"

"Why would I hate you?"

"I don't know, but with my track record, I'm a little leery planning too far in advance."

With her hands on the cart, he moved behind her and pushed her and the cart toward the furniture.

"Time to make a decision," he said.

"Should I include David?"

"No," he said. "He doesn't care as long as the baby is safe."

They walked to the furniture aisle and gazed at all the cribs, rockers, changing tables, and chests.

"Oh, I like this one," she said. "What do you think?"

A woman came up to them. "Look at you. When are you due?"

"The end of October," she said.

Then she turned to Tyler. "Are you excited?"

"More than words can express," he said and gazed at Crystal, who was trying to keep from laughing.

"Is this your first?"

"Yes," Crystal said, thinking *and her last* unless something changed.

"Congratulations, you two. You look so in love," the woman said, walking off.

They both turned and stared at one another.

"That's awkward," Crystal said.

Tyler grinned. "Doesn't have to be."

He pulled her into his arms, the baby keeping them from being too close.

"People are going to assume what they want about us. Today, I'm the happy expectant father."

"You play the role well," Crystal said.

"Thank you. Enough for an Academy Award?"

"Hmm, not quite," she reached up and ran her fingers down his cheek in a caress. "I don't even know if you want children or like them?"

"Of course, I want children. I've just never found the right person," he said. "After witnessing so many divorces, I'm wary. I only want to marry once."

"Me too," she said. "And now I doubt I will ever marry. And I never want an engagement again."

Laughing, he leaned in and kissed her on the lips. "Come on, let's decide on the furniture and then move on to the next aisle. We've still got a long way to go and a movie is waiting on us."

"Yes," she said. "Thank you for today."

Two hours later, they left the store. She purchased the furniture to be delivered in thirty days, plus some little outfits she thought were adorable to take her son home from the hospital in or to wear when they went out.

"This is everything I'd dreamed it would be like with a husband by my side," she said. "Thank you for being the stand-in today."

"You're welcome," he said his voice gruff.

When they arrived at the movie theater, he bought her popcorn and a Coke. Sitting in the theater, he held her hand and she felt like a queen. Afterward, they walked out and she sighed.

"Today has been fun. Would you mind if we ordered takeout and took it back to the house? I'm getting tired and my feet feel like they're swelling."

Glancing down, he frowned. "The next time you go see Dr. Jane, you need to mention this."

"I'm pregnant. It's what happens to fat pregnant women," she said.

"You're not fat, and frankly, I find you extremely beautiful," he said as he opened the car door. "Let's get you home. But I would love if we could sneak out and have a late-night stroll on the beach."

"Me too," she said. "Let's get my feet propped up and then we'll go."

Pulling her as close as he could, his lips covered hers and his tongue swept through her mouth sending sensations spiraling through her.

A moan escaped from her lips. "You're making it extremely hard not to have sex with you."

He grinned. "That's my job."

"You're awfully good at it," she said as he helped her into the seat.

"I'm glad you like it," he said.

And she did. When he touched her, a rush of passion spiraled through her and left her gasping and wanting more. The man was so handsome and yet she was so pregnant.

Sitting in the car, she had never felt happier with a man. Tyler made her feel like the luckiest woman alive.

When he sank into the driver's seat, she reached over for his hand. She wanted to touch him, to feel his skin against hers. She wanted Tyler in the worst possible way, but it didn't feel right. Not with her belly sticking out and her feet and ankles swelling.

Not when she was pregnant with David's child.

CHAPTER 21

"Hello, ladies," David said as he walked into the family room where they were holding her baby shower.

The women told her that they thought it would be a wonderful place to have her party and she wouldn't have to leave home. But they would set up everything.

She was excited to see what the baby was going to receive.

"Hello," the women replied.

It was only a handful of others – her friends and ladies she worked with. In all, there were about eight women attending, plus Tyler and David.

They had been having secret meetings and whispering, so they must have been doing something to surprise her. The very thought of them doing this was special. Since her parents' death, she'd not experienced such closeness or such warmth.

"Okay, ladies and gentlemen, we're going to play baby shower games," Amanda said.

SYLVIA MCDANIEL

"What have you gotten me dragged into," Tyler said, gazing at David.

"Oh, come on, women can't have all the fun. I'm the father, I should be here," he said.

There was a gasp, and she realized these women didn't know who the father of her child was.

"We're keeping that information quiet until the baby is born," Crystal said, glancing around at the women, hoping none of them would sell their story to the tabloids.

"Congratulations," one of her employees said smiling. "I'm so happy for you."

"What's the game?" David said.

Today, she noted he was feeling good and she wanted him to enjoy this as much as she was going to.

"Pin the pacifier on the baby," Jennifer said.

"Tyler, you're up first," Nicole said and put the blindfold on him.

"No wonder I thought Crystal was crazy. Look at her friends."

They spun him around and handed him a Binky to put on the baby's face. He put it on the baby's cheek.

"David is next," Nicole said.

The man stood. "I think I can do better than you."

"You're going to be lucky not to put it in the baby's eye," Tyler told him.

Crystal sat back and watched. At eight months, she was beginning to feel tired. Though it was only September, she was ready to hold the baby. Spinning her around was not a good idea.

After they spun David, he put the pacifier in the baby's nose.

One by one, the women took a turn with Lucy winning.

"Next, we're playing the blindfolded diaper challenge. We're going to see who can put a diaper on blindfolded the best and the fastest. We have a stopwatch ready, and here are the babies," Jennifer said. "We're going to do this two at a time. You're competing against one another. David and Tyler as our only men, you go first."

"I got this," Tyler told David. "I'm going to show you how it's done, blindfolded."

David picked up the baby and it cried. "I'm already ahead of you. My baby is crying because he's wet."

Jennifer slipped the blindfolds on both men.

"Don't start until I say go," she said watching them. "Go."

The women watched as they couldn't find the diapers at first. Then David picked his up and turned to Tyler and tried to put it on him.

"Hey, I'm not the baby," he said with the women giggling.

"I just thought I'd try," David told him.

The women were rolling with laughter as they watched the two men try to put the diaper on. At three minutes, Tyler turned toward Jennifer.

"I'm done," he said, yanking the blindfold off.

The diaper was on the baby, but he had two legs in one hole, which was the waist. David removed his blindfold and his baby had the diaper on correctly.

"Turtle wins the race," he said, grinning at his friend.

Crystal's heart filled with love as she watched these two men. They shared a bond that she couldn't imagine having with anyone else. And with Tyler, she was falling in love.

Who would've thought she would go for the jerk next door

on the cruise? Who would've thought fate would bring them together again?

"We've got one thing to do before we open presents," Amanda said. "We thought it would be fun for everyone to decorate a onesie for the baby. I've got paints and patterns, and if you want to put a special message on it, you can. We thought it would be best to do this outside on the patio."

The women moved to the exterior, David and Tyler following.

The ladies were giggly as they chose their pattern and the color of the fabric paint they wanted to use. Quickly, the designs began to take shape and she was amazed at some of the designs. Some of her friends were very artistic.

Once everyone was finished, Jennifer picked up the first little onesie. "A bat and ball design with the saying below. *Life is a game. Enjoy.*"

"Aww," the group of women cooed.

Amanda picked up a little shirt with a turtle on it. "Grow slow and enjoy the ride."

They went around the table until they got to David's. He had freehand drawn a game controller on it. "Win."

Last was Tyler's. "Dang, I'm not as artsy as all of you."

Jennifer laughed as she held up the tiny shirt with a baby bottle on it. Below the bottle was *DUI? Call Tyler Nelson.*

"Tyler," Crystal said, laughing.

"Well, he has my contact info if he needs me."

The women traipsed back into the house where Maria handed out drinks with ice cubes with tiny plastic babies inside them.

"Our last game is whoever's baby ice cube melts first is to

yell, 'My water broke!'" Nicole told the group while Amanda started handing the gifts to Crystal to open.

Tears blossomed in her eyes as she opened the things she had put on her list at the baby store. With each gift, the realization that this was happening overwhelmed her.

Glancing at David, she could tell he was having a good time. And she was grateful that today was a wonderful day for him.

When she unwrapped a swing, he smiled. "You said you wanted one of those."

"Yes, Jennifer told me they came in handy," she said.

After she'd opened the last gift, she realized she hadn't received anything from Tyler or David and she felt disappointed.

David stood. "Ladies, would you please blindfold Crystal."

"What?"

They stood her up and she realized they were in on whatever he had planned. She felt his hand and Tyler's on her. Walking through the house, they led her up the stairs.

Tyler removed the blindfold and she saw that the bedroom had balloons and decorations on the door.

"Open the door, Crystal," David said.

She glanced at him and then at Tyler. "What have you guys done?"

"Open the door," Tyler said.

Pushing open the door, she saw the most fabulous nursery. The furniture she had picked out was all set up, including a rocker she had not purchased, but said she wanted. The walls were painted in a light blue, not the orange she had teased Tyler about.

"Oh my," she said. "It's all ready except for his little clothes."

David turned to her and took her hands. "This has been the most magical journey and I can't wait to see our son."

Tears filled her eyes and she threw her arms around him, feeling the bones beneath his shirt. He'd lost weight and was getting worse by the day. Every night, she prayed he would last one more month.

"Thank you," she cried. "You've been so good to me."

Today was a good day. Turning, she glanced at Tyler, tears streaming down her cheeks.

"The small wooden crib you can put by your bed at night," Tyler said. "I made that for you."

Warmth filled her as she turned and hugged him. His gift was so personal. "Thank you."

"There's one other thing," David said, handing her an envelope.

Glancing at him, she opened the envelope and read how her son now had his own college education fund that had over a hundred thousand dollars in it.

"David, that's too much," she said.

"No, we don't know what college will cost in eighteen years. Plus, this will give him a little spending money."

Her son's education was all taken care of and she couldn't feel more blessed.

Suddenly Jennifer yelled. "My water broke."

They all turned to her to see her lift her glass and the plastic baby floating free of the cube of ice and laughed.

When they went back downstairs, Crystal stood before the women.

"Thank you for making this day special for me and our

son. It means so much that you were all here. Each of your presents is a special gift and I loved the onesies. Again, thank you for being my friend and celebrating the birth of our son."

The women began to leave except for her good friends who helped clean up so Maria didn't have to do it all.

Finally, they came in and sat with Crystal. David had disappeared, probably to rest, and Tyler was there by her side as she reclined on the couch, her feet propped up.

"Thank you, ladies. I love you all," she said.

Jennifer hugged her. "We're so happy for you. I can't believe that your other wedding was almost a year ago. The one we kept telling you not to do, and thank God, you didn't marry him."

That felt like a hundred years ago. "But because of me running away from that wedding, I made the decision to have a child. And here I am pregnant with David's child."

"And she met me on the cruise," Tyler said, gazing at her with so much emotion in his eyes.

She couldn't wait for everyone to leave and for them to take their nightly stroll down the beach.

"Things happen in life for a reason," Amanda said. "Thank you, Tyler. You got me a very nice settlement. Enough that I can do what I want."

He smiled. "Well, he made it rather easy."

She grinned. "Never thought I would be divorced, but here we are, and I'm learning to accept it."

Jennifer hugged Amanda. "It gets easier."

"I'm not going to be the dried-up, old, hateful, divorced woman living on the beach. I may shock all of you and become that dazzling divorcee."

SYLVIA MCDANIEL

"You go, girl," Crystal said. "He's so going to regret losing you."

"Doubtful since he's already dating. At this time, I'll just say I hope he gets everything he deserves."

"Bless his heart," Nicole said.

The women all laughed.

"This month is the hardest," Amanda said. "If you need anything at all, even someone just to talk to, call me."

The women all stood to leave and Crystal hugged them. "I will and when the time comes, I'll have Tyler let you know," she said.

Amanda laid her hand on her arm. "What about David? He looked good today."

She glanced at Tyler, not wanting to say too much.

"We're just taking it one day at a time and praying that he's here for the birth of the baby. Thanks again, my friends. I don't know what I would do without all of you."

"Oh, just wait," Amanda said. "You'll be calling us crying in several months, wanting to know when the midnight feedings end and if you can sleep through the night."

"I can't wait," Crystal told them as they walked out the door. "Goodnight."

After they left, she turned to Tyler. "Thank you for making today special."

"Thanks for including David and me. It was fun, and I think it did him so much good."

"Me too. Now, Mr. Nelson, you owe me a walk on the beach and then more dessert. I'm craving another piece of that cake with a big dollop of ice cream on it."

Leaning down, he kissed her. "My pleasure."

166

CHAPTER 22

*I*t was hurricane season and thankfully this year, so far, they had not had any major storms. Not like last year when a category three hurricane came ashore not far from Corpus.

Sitting on the deck, David gazed out at the ocean. His days were numbered and he knew it. Every day his body seemed to grow more fragile, and yet his will to live was strong.

He wanted to see his son.

Crystal was in the last month and she grew tired much quicker. Her cheerful personality was still there, but her feet swelled on a daily basis, and she and Tyler had stopped their evening walks along the beach.

His greatest wish besides seeing his son born was that the two of them would fall in love and marry. But, regardless, he knew for certain that Tyler would look out for Crystal and the boy.

Tonight, he would tell them his decision. He had fought so long and hard not to succumb, but it was time. Time to call hospice. Time for him to admit that he needed help with bathing and sometimes even walking.

The doctor had warned him that he would need help, but he hadn't wanted to give in to the need. Now it was time. In fact, he'd called him this morning. He'd also hired a full-time nurse to help him during the day.

He didn't want to die. He wanted to live, and yet his body was declining. Giving out on him.

His time grew short, but he still had several things he wanted to do. Mainly, another will change, but this time, Tyler would not be involved. There were things he wanted in the will that involved him. Things, he wasn't ready to reveal.

The ocean waves broke hard against the shore, sending peaceful vibes through him. A tropical storm churned in the gulf, but it wasn't expected to become a hurricane. The surf was higher than normal and the storm out at sea was giving them a spectacular show of the waves' power.

Glancing at the water, he wondered if there was a heaven. He'd lived a good life and yet he wasn't certain if there was an afterlife. He guessed that soon he would find out.

After witnessing so much of the earth, he believed in God and knew that he had created the wonders he'd seen, but he just wasn't certain there was a place that spirits went to after leaving the body.

With a sigh, he stood and a wave of dizziness overcame him. The doctor had given him the signs and told him that, eventually, he would be confined to bed, but not yet. Please not yet.

The videos for his son's future were done, and even though he would not know if his son watched them or not, at least the opportunity was there. He'd even recorded one on his life, showing pictures of him as a baby through now. But with his body rapidly declining, he didn't want his son to see him in his last days.

The dizziness passed and he took a step toward the house. Time to tell his friends of his decision. Time to let them know that he wouldn't be here much longer.

Since he stopped chemo, he had resigned himself to death. There was no escaping the end.

But, damn, he wanted to see his son, hold him in his arms and kiss his sweet baby cheek. Then he could go peacefully, knowing he'd secured his future and fought until the end.

CHAPTER 23

This past week, Crystal had a resurgence of her energy. She'd washed and folded all the baby clothes and made certain that her bag was packed and ready to go in case they had to go to the hospital.

Dr. Jane had told her she was right on time, and they had decided to have the baby at home. Her pregnancy had been good with little or no complications, and even though a hospital was safer, traveling had become extremely difficult for David and she wanted him beside her along with Tyler.

So now they were all set up for home delivery and even Dr. Jane said she would come to the house to deliver their boy. She and David had been friends long before Crystal met her.

The baby felt like it was sitting on her bladder and she had to pee every thirty minutes it seemed. And she had better not wait or she would be in trouble. As much as she'd enjoyed being pregnant, she was ready for her son to be born.

David had grown weaker. He seemed to sleep most of the

day, and when he did get up, sometimes he was too weak to walk.

Tyler and she worried more and more that he wasn't going to see his son born. A full-time nurse now took care of David.

She spent her day elated that it was almost time for her son to be born and sad that David was losing his battle. Sad that her friend was slowly wasting away.

Last night, she thought she had mild contractions, but she wasn't certain. Tyler had sat beside her and they timed them. But then they stopped and, disappointed, he held her until she fell asleep.

A week ago, he started to sleep in her bed in case she needed him during the night. It was both exhilarating and terrifying.

She trusted him to keep his word that they would not have sex. And as large as she was, she didn't think it would even be possible, but it was emotionally terrifying.

Since June, they had been close, kissing, and had even gone skinny dipping in the ocean a couple of times, but they turned their back when they got out of the water.

She wasn't ready and the thought of committing to him panicked her. What if she chose the wrong person again? What if she was brokenhearted once more?

This morning, her back ached as she rose from bed, then she took a shower and went down to breakfast.

Today was Tyler's day to go into the office and he'd left early this morning. There was no sign of David, who was probably still asleep. Maria was already in the kitchen making lunch or dinner or something special.

"Would you like some breakfast?" Maria asked, gazing at her. "Are you all right?"

"I think so," she said. "My back is killing me."

"That baby looks like he's about to crawl out," she said. "Are you having contractions?"

"I don't think so," she said, recalling what it had felt like last night.

She picked up her phone to see a text from Tyler. *I'm in meetings most of the day, but if you need me, call my secretary. She's been told that if you call, she's to come and get me.*

There were kiss emojis and a pregnant lady emoji and she couldn't help but smile.

"Maybe you should skip breakfast this morning," Maria said. "I'm worried that you're going to go into labor any moment."

"I'm fine," she told Maria. "Though I think I'm ready for this to be over."

The woman grinned at her.

She really wasn't hungry and the thought of skipping breakfast sounded good. She stood and waddled to the deck. Maybe she could take a walk on the beach. She wouldn't go far.

Stepping outside onto the sand, she breathed in the fresh ocean air and noticed the surf was calm this morning. She headed toward the water and skimmed the surf line.

The sun shined brightly on this late October day, and she couldn't help but think about her mother. Oh, how she wished her mom was here to help her through the delivery and the first few weeks of being a parent. She was a little scared now that it was so near.

She was frightened that she would do something wrong. That she would harm the baby with her lack of knowledge, even though she'd read about ten pregnancy and child rearing books.

She wanted to be a good mother to her son. Already she loved him and couldn't wait to hold him.

A sharp pain radiated in her back and she gasped. Water ran *down* her legs and she stared as she realized her water had just broken. She was in labor.

As soon as the pain eased, she eased toward the house. Before she reached the door, it happened again. The pain radiated in her back and moved to her pelvis. It lasted about forty-five seconds.

They were about five minutes apart.

When she entered the house, she went upstairs and cleaned up. Bam, it hit her again and she breathed through the contraction knowing instinctively that this was not Braxton Hicks. She was in labor.

Her son was going to be born today.

When she'd changed her clothes, she picked up her cell phone and called Tyler's secretary.

"Hello, this is Crystal," she said. "Tell Tyler that my water has broken and I'm having contractions about every five minutes."

The secretary gasped. "Oh my, goodness. I'll go get him right now. Good luck."

"Thank you," she said and then she dialed the doctor and gave the nurse the same news.

The nurse said, "I'll give her the message. Are you on your way to the hospital?"

"No, I'm delivering at home," she said.

"Good luck," the young girl replied.

One of the things she read about being in labor was to get

up and walk. So she began to pace her bedroom. Then she remembered Maria.

"Maria," she hollered. The woman came running up the stairs, her face white and her eyes wide. "I'm in labor," she said. "My water broke and I'm having contractions."

"Oh no," she said.

"I've called Tyler and the doctor," she said. "So they should be arriving soon. Is David up?"

Pacing the floor now, she knew the next contraction should be coming soon.

"Ugh," she cried as the contraction hit her and she breathed through it trying to remain calm wanting someone she loved near her.

"Breathe," Maria coached.

As soon as it passed, she rested. This was just the beginning. From what she'd read, contractions would come faster and stronger until the baby was born.

Understanding that first babies arrived on their schedule, she wondered when her son would be born.

Glancing at her watch, she counted down to the next knife stab in the back. Just as it hit, the bedroom door swung open and David walked through. He and Tyler both had gone to the birthing classes with her and he took her hand.

"Breathe," he told her and she relaxed as much as she could to follow through with the techniques they had been taught. Turning his wrist, he timed it.

When it was over, he smiled. "Fifty seconds long. Have you called Dr. Jane?"

"Yes," she said. "And Tyler too."

"It's early," he said, still gazing at his watch.

"Yes," she replied as she walked the length of her bedroom

and back. *Keep walking. Keep concentrating on how soon your son will be born.*

The next contraction came in four and a half minutes. They were already getting shorter and stronger.

Suddenly the door burst open and Tyler came rushing in. "What's going on?"

"We're having a baby," David said. "She's having contractions every four and a half minutes."

He hugged her and kissed her on the cheek. "Are you doing all right?"

"So far," she said.

"Is Dr. Jane on the way?"

"I called her office," she said.

The two men stared at her as she paced the floor.

"Shouldn't you be lying in bed?" Tyler asked.

"No, it's better if I walk," she replied.

An hour later, she really hurt. She knew there would come a point when it would become painful, but she hadn't expected it so soon. What if she had hours to go? Some women were in labor for twenty hours or more. She couldn't do this that long.

What if something was wrong?

"Tyler," she cried just as another contraction seized her. The pain had moved from her lower back, radiating around to the front and low in her groin area.

"What do you need? Remember those exercises we learned," he said, holding her hand.

"Fuck those exercises. This is starting to get serious," she said.

He laughed. "Come on, Crystal, they promised proper breathing would help. Now do it with me."

Dr. Jane's nurse walked in the door and smiled at her. "You're in labor."

The contraction had her trapped and she nodded. Finally it ended, and the nurse started her watch. "Dr. Jane will be here very soon. First babies are often slow, so I'm here to be with you until she arrives."

Crystal sank onto the bed.

"Now, gentlemen, I know you're going to be here for the birth, but can you walk outside while I examine Crystal and we talk for a few moments."

The men glanced at her and she nodded. She really didn't want them to see the nurse checking out her lady bits to see if they were ready.

The nurse had her lie back on the bed and that left her back aching.

"Look at you, you're already dilated to a seven. When did your contractions start?"

Crystal told her just as another contraction hit her.

"Wow, that was four minutes between contractions. I'm going to let the men back in and then I'm going to call Dr. Jane and tell her how far you've progressed."

With a gasp when the contraction ended, she asked, "How much longer?"

"Wish I could tell you, but you're already at seven and babies arrive once you reach ten. So we still have a ways to go," she said, lowering Crystal's maternity dress, and then went to the door. "Walking is a good way to help labor along."

Crystal nodded, not wanting to move, but if it would end this sooner, then she would walk.

David and Tyler rushed in, their faces a mix of excitement and worry.

"The nurse told us you're at a seven," David said, light sparkling in his eyes.

Tyler grinned at her. "Maybe your Braxton Hicks last night were really the start of your labor."

She nodded just as another one hit her. When it was over, she sighed. "Maria wouldn't feed me any breakfast this morning because she thought I looked like I was in labor. And apparently I was."

The men turned and glanced at one another smiling.

For the next two hours, the contractions became stronger, and she wondered if she could do this. Doubts swirled when her thoughts weren't blown away by agony.

Tyler did his best to make her smile while David just kept telling her she was doing great. No, she wasn't doing great. This baby was a little monster who was going to kill her.

Another hour passed and then Dr. Jane walked in. She put on a gown and gloves and had Crystal lie back on the bed.

"You're doing great. That little boy is almost ready to meet his new family."

Tears welled in her eyes. "I'm going to make it."

"Crystal, you're doing great. You're almost ready. When you're completely dilated, the contractions may stop. Some women experience what is called the *rest and be thankful* phase. They get some time to rest before they begin again. If that happens, we just wait. If not, you'll feel the need to push."

The contractions felt like they were one on top of the other.

"Who is going to help her deliver?" the doctor asked.

"Me," Tyler said. "David will be down at her feet, I'm going to lift her up."

"It's time," Dr. Jane said.

"I need to push," Crystal screamed.

Tyler raised her into a sitting position and she pushed with a grunt. It was almost over. Soon she would see her son and get to rest.

"Come on, Crystal, push," Dr. Jane said. "I can see his head crowning. Your son is about to enter this world."

Closing her eyes, she gave it her all and felt his head burst through and then slip out of her body. Opening her eyes, she stared down at the red, messy baby.

David was bawling his eyes out, and Tyler had tears running down his cheeks, but all she could do was look at her son. He was here.

"Look at him," Dr. Jane said. "A healthy baby boy who is looking around to see what is going on."

She gave him a little pat on the butt and he began to cry. "That's what I need to hear. Listen to those healthy lungs. David, would you like to cut the umbilical cord?" The nurse placed two clamps on the cord.

Unable to speak, he nodded and she handed him the umbilical scissors. "You can't hurt him or Crystal as long you cut between the clamps."

Quickly, he snipped the cord.

Turning the baby onto his stomach, the doctor laid him on Crystal. "Meet your momma. You can rest here just a moment while I take care of the afterbirth. Then the nurse will need to take some measurements. Then you're free to hold your new son."

They all stared in amazement at the tiny human lying on her stomach.

"Look at that hair," Crystal said. "He has almost a full head."

The doctor laughed.

The baby's hand clasped and unclasped and she reached down and touched his fingers with hers. "Welcome to the world, son."

The nurse scooped the newborn off her stomach. "Sorry, little man, but I need to clean you up and take some measurements."

Five minutes later, she brought the baby back to Crystal who took her son into her arms, her heart swelling with so much love, she thought she would die.

She kissed his forehead, tears streaming down her cheeks. "He's beautiful."

Then she glanced at David. "Tyler, take the baby and let David hold his son."

The man sobbed as Tyler placed the baby in his arms. He leaned down and kissed him on the cheek.

"Oh, he's so tiny and so handsome," he sobbed.

The baby gazed up at him and raised his tiny fist to his mouth.

"I'm so glad to meet you," he said. "And I'm sorry I won't be here to watch you grow into a man."

Crystal sobbed while Tyler cried, and even the nurse and doctor wiped away tears.

"I love you," David said. "I've loved you from the moment you were conceived."

CHAPTER 24

*T*he next few days were joyful as they celebrated the birth of David Wayne Avara. Crystal was doing well, though she'd had some soreness. But she was adjusting to the baby's schedule and Tyler loved watching her breastfeed the baby.

David had smiled at the name she'd chosen and they all had been overwhelmed with emotion these last several days.

Tyler had not moved out of her room. He liked sleeping beside her. She even eased his insomnia. He loved being with her and he wanted to tell her he loved her.

This woman amazed him and he didn't know why and how he hadn't seen her unique, loving personality that night on the ship.

They were so close and he even awoke when she got up for the late-night feedings. He woke when the baby cried, changed his diaper, and then handed him to Crystal. This baby had created a special bond between them that he never wanted to see end.

And, yes, he was David's son, but Tyler still loved him like his own.

Part of him wanted to ask her to marry him. She was the only woman he'd ever become this close to, but then he would remember how his own family had been. When his father died, the family had changed, and not for the better.

He feared dying and leaving behind a family. Look what was happening with David. What if that happened to him? What if he was suddenly taken and he was married and had children? That would leave Crystal to raise them alone.

And he knew firsthand what that experience was like. It was not good.

Even today, his mother and sister were still arguing over something ridiculous. And yet he only thought of Crystal. He wanted to be with her every moment he could.

But she also had ghosts in the closet that she had never told him about. She'd also lost her parents and a sibling. For her, it seemed to drive her to want to recreate what she'd lost.

He had very few memories of his father, but the ones he had were great. And there were so many times he wished he was still here.

When he first went to law school, he looked up his father's killer and visited him in prison. There, Tyler told the man how he'd destroyed his family, and how he'd lost a great father because of him.

The man had gotten up and walked away. The man had thought Tyler was coming to help him get out of jail, but he was wrong. One hundred percent wrong. If he had his way, the man would have gotten life in jail without parole ever.

Driving home from work, he was eager to see Crystal and hold the baby. He was keen to spend as much time with David as he could. The man was declining by the day and would not be here much longer.

But the days that he was here, he spent with the baby and Crystal and Tyler. In fact, Tyler was not going to return to work until January. He'd told the office he had a new baby and a friend that was dying. He needed personal time off.

Since David was the firm's biggest client, his bosses readily conceded.

As he pulled up in front of the house, he noticed several cars parked outside.

A smile spread across his face remembering Crystal's friends. They were here to see the baby.

When he walked into the house, they were gathered in the family room. Jennifer was holding the baby who had his eyes open and gazing up at her.

"Hi," they called out as a group.

"Isn't he the cutest baby ever," Tyler said. He leaned down and kissed him on the forehead.

"This from the man who told David not to do this," Crystal said with a grin.

"A good attorney always tells their client what could go wrong and there could have been so much that went sideways with this."

"It was the best decision I've made," David said.

Tyler couldn't agree more. This had turned out much better than he thought possible. The only hiccup was that David wouldn't be here much longer. Glancing at Crystal, oh, how he wanted to lean in and kiss her. But her friends were here. David was watching, and though he knew his friend was suspicious, he didn't care. Soon he would sit down with him and tell him his feelings regarding Crystal.

David sat in his wheelchair watching everyone. Sometimes he appeared like he was participating in the conversation, but other times, he had a distant look in his gaze. God, he was going to miss his friend so much. There was nothing he could do but accept David was going to die.

"How are you feeling?" Tyler asked Crystal.

"I'm doing better every day," she said.

Looking around, he found Amanda. "How are you?"

She grinned. "I'm doing much better. Thank you."

"Glad to hear you're doing all right," he said. The woman's divorce had been extremely hard on her. After being married for twenty-five years and then your husband wanted to split, it couldn't be easy.

Crystal made room for him on the couch and he sat.

"My turn to hold him," Amanda said, taking the baby from Jennifer.

For the next hour, they passed around the infant until finally, David got up and took him from Nicole.

"Time for me and little man to spend our nightly time together. If you'll excuse us," he said and the nurse rolled the wheelchair into his room.

The women all stared in shock.

"He does this every evening. It's called father-and-son hour and as long as he can do it, I'm happy."

Jennifer shook her head. "He's not looking good."

"No, he's not," Nicole replied. "Are you sure you should leave the baby alone with him?"

Tyler stepped in. "The nurse is with him and this gives Crystal a break."

Amanda nodded. "That's wonderful. I have five kids and

no alone time. None. How we had so many kids I will never understand."

The women stood and glanced at each other.

"I think we should go. We've kept Miss Crystal up way too long. She needs her rest," Amanda said.

"When you're well, we'll come back and spoil that baby as much as we're allowed," Nicole said.

"Enjoy him as much as you can because soon he'll be eighteen and going off to college," Jennifer told her.

Tyler saw the women to the door. "Thanks for coming by, ladies. I know this means so much to Crystal," he said.

"You take good care of her," Amanda said. "I think you two would make a great couple. And she's going to need support when David goes."

"I'm going to need some myself when that happens," Tyler admitted.

"Goodnight," they called as they walked to their cars.

When he went back in, Crystal was still on the couch. "Hold me," she said.

"Any time," he replied. "Are you all right?"

"I'm fine. Hormones are a little on the wonky side, but I think about Baby David and know I'm so blessed."

He lifted her mouth to his and kissed her. It wasn't a passionate kiss, but just a simple smooch to remind her that he was here for her.

"When you're feeling better, I want us to go on a real date again," he said, wanting to get even closer to her.

"Who will keep Baby David?"

That was a good question.

"I don't want to leave him with anyone I don't trust. David

is not strong enough to keep him and Maria could, but would she want to?"

This was going to be an issue, especially if he wanted time with her alone. Maybe he could find a nanny she would trust.

She ran her hand down his face in a caress that left him breathless.

"I understand, but I want to be with you," he said.

"Maybe we can soon start up our walks along the beach," she said. "I could take the baby monitor and we could hear him if he cries."

Leaning down, he kissed her again.

"Crystal, this thing between us is growing stronger," he said.

"Yes," she said. "Let me get well and then we'll go out to dinner if we can find someone to sit with Baby David."

Warmth filled him. "All right."

"You know who might enjoy watching him is Amanda. And she knows how to take care of babies," she said.

That was an excellent idea. "Yes. And we can have an evening alone."

She smiled. "I would like that."

CHAPTER 25

*T*he baby was almost a month old and starting to recognize faces and make little cooing noises. He was a happy baby as long as he was fed, but he didn't like missing a meal and Crystal was breastfeeding him constantly.

David knew that he would soon be gone. Every day he lost strength and the ability to do little things for himself. The oncologist was right when he said David would not be here at Christmas.

But his shopping was done and his presents were wrapped and Maria would put them under the tree. His nurse took good care of him and made certain he received his medications on time along with the pain meds which were needed now more than ever.

He didn't want to spend his last days in a drug-induced coma, but sometimes he needed help to handle the pain.

Everything was ready except for one last thing on his list. And he wasn't certain if would get his last wish, but he wanted to try.

This morning, he went in search of Tyler and found him on his computer.

"Let's go for a walk," David said, knowing he couldn't go far and that he would tire before long.

"All right," Tyler said, jumping up.

They walked down to the water. "I have loved living here."

Tyler smiled. "I'm just glad that Crystal, the baby, and myself are here with you. We love living here with you."

"I'm glad," David said.

"When you start feeling tired, let me know," Tyler said, walking slowly.

One of the disadvantages of becoming ill was losing your strength and stamina. David wanted to run along the beach like he did years ago, but that wasn't possible.

"I will," he said. "I know you and Crystal are sharing the same bedroom. How do you feel about her?"

Tyler smiled. "This started back in the summer. We tried to hide it from you because we didn't want to get your hopes up. I'm going to ask her to dinner next week and there I'm going to tell her I love her."

He smiled. "I'm so happy. Are you going to ask her to marry you?"

Tyler frowned and David noted some reservations. "I've never considered marriage, not after what happened to my father. Being raised in an all-female house was not a good place to be."

"I understand," David said. "We've talked before about how the death of your father affected you. My sweet boy will be raised in a female home."

"That was one of the reasons why I tried to stop you,"

Tyler said. "Are you questioning whether or not Crystal will be a good mother?"

"No," David said, wondering how he could make the man see what he wanted without saying the words aloud. "Crystal is an excellent mother. I'm thrilled that I chose her. But I see you and her together and I wonder why you don't just marry."

Tyler tensed and David could see that he wasn't open to the idea of marriage, not even to Crystal.

"I'm sorry, I'm intruding. It's just I see the affection you have for one another and thought you two would be a great pair to raise my son. I thought maybe you loved her enough to put a ring on her finger."

The water came up and splashed over their feet. It was cold, but he didn't care. At least he could feel the waves coming onto the shore.

"I love her, David, I do, but I just fear that something would happen to me, just like it's happening to you, and I'd leave her behind with a house full of children and no man to make them behave," he said.

David laughed. "And you think that if your father had been there that your family dynamics would've been different?"

"Yes, maybe he could have stopped my mother and sister from fighting all time," he said, remembering the night he had to take a knife from his sister's hand. She was ready to kill their mother.

"And they still fight to this day?"

"Yes," he said, recalling the memories of the cruise he'd gone on with them and how that was the last family vacation he wanted any part of.

"So what are you going to do? Just live with her? Or are you going to walk away and break her heart?"

There was silence as they walked slowly along the beach.

"I don't know. I was going to tell her I love her when I took her out to dinner, but you're right. She deserves a man who is willing to marry her and I don't know if I'm that man," he said.

"You've been living with her for a while now. How is it going to feel not to see her every day? Not to play with Baby David? Not to be by her side?"

Tyler closed his eyes. "I don't know. I don't have an answer for you."

"I'm tired. We need to turn around and go back," David said, his heart aching. How could his friend be such a fool? How could he not be willing to commit all because of his mother and sister?

Everyone had something in their past. Everyone, including him. And now how he regretted not following his heart.

They were silent on the way back and David was exhausted. He went inside his room and crawled into bed. Before he talked to Crystal, he had to rest.

Three hours later, he went in search of her. She was feeding the baby and he watched as she let him suckle at her breast.

"Hey, you, are you here for your time with Baby David?"

"Yes, but first I want to talk to you," he said. "What is going on between you and Tyler?"

A smile crossed her face. "I love him, David. Over these last few months, I've fallen for him. He's been there by my side and taken care of me. He makes me laugh and I love how he is with Baby David."

"Me too," David said. "I just wanted to know what you felt for him."

"I'm afraid of getting engaged again. I'm a three-time loser, but I don't feel any doubts about Tyler."

"Have you told him?"

"No," she said. "Life kind of interfered and we haven't had a chance to be alone and really talk."

He smiled thinking maybe she should be feeling some doubts, knowing his friend was afraid, but he kept his mouth shut.

"I just want you to be happy," he said.

"And I am," she replied. "My heart breaks thinking about you leaving us, but I love this little boy more than I thought humanly possible. And Tyler, I love him and I love you. My heart is full right now."

"I love you, Crystal. You've given me what I wanted and I can't thank you enough," he said, running his hand over his son's brow.

She raised the baby onto her shoulder and let him give a loud burp. The baby's eyes were closed and he was sound asleep.

"He's growing," she said. "I think he's gained several pounds. His next pediatrician appointment is next week. Do you want to come?"

Yes, he wanted to go, but he didn't know if he would have the strength to leave the house.

"We'll see," he said. "What if I watch him while you go find Tyler and walk along the beach? I know you guys like to do that in the evenings."

Crystal smiled at him, "Thank you."

She made certain the baby had a fresh diaper and then she went in search of Tyler.

David took the small baby crib out onto the deck where he could watch to see if his final wish would come true. Covering the crib with a blanket, he sat in a chair and hoped he would see these two realize they couldn't live without one another.

CHAPTER 26

Tyler sat on the deck, watching the ocean and thinking about his conversation with David this morning. Was he the biggest fool in the universe?

Crystal wasn't his mother, who could be the most trying woman on the planet. And his sister was just as bad. They were alike and that's why they fought like they did.

As soon as he'd graduated from high school, he'd gotten out of that situation and gone to college. After that, he'd never moved back home.

Was he wrong to fear being married? And yet he'd never felt as much emotion for a woman as he had with Crystal. He'd seen her at her worst and at her best and he still loved her.

"Want to go for a walk," Crystal asked as she came out the door.

"Yes," he said, rising from the lounge chair, wanting to be with her.

"What a beautiful evening," she said as they walked along the sand.

"Yes," he said with a sigh. "We've never talked about our past. You've never told me about your family and I've never told you about mine. Why not?"

There was silence for several moments. "I was in college. It was Parent's Day. My family had come to visit me and they brought my little sister with them. We spent the day doing the activities and then they left for home. We hugged and said good-bye and my father told me to keep my grades up. My mother told me to be a good girl and how she was so proud of me. My sister teased me and said she couldn't wait to go to college.

"They left and on the way home, a drunk crossed the center line of the road. He hit them head-on, doing close to one hundred. All three of them were killed."

She took a deep breath and sighed. The pain of that night still felt fresh and raw. Her chest seized at the thought of them, and she felt anger that they would never know her son. "Later that night, my dorm mother called me downstairs to speak to two policemen. Standing there in shock, I got the usual, *we regret to inform you...*"

Tyler had read the background report and he knew this, but to hear it coming from her was so much more painful.

"I was nineteen years old. Nineteen when I filed suit against the driver's insurance, his family, the bar, everyone I could. That wasn't his first offense. He had two previous DUIs, plus, he'd been to rehab several times. He would never drive again, but I wanted the people who let him get behind the wheel to feel the pain I felt."

They walked on as the water rolled over her feet.

"The money paid for my education, but it never healed the hole in my heart. It never replaced the people I lost. With no

SYLVIA MCDANIEL

aunts or uncles or even cousins, I was all alone in the world. It was why I wanted a family of my own so badly. Only I have this terrible tendency to pick the wrong men."

His family life was not good, but at least he had people who loved him.

"The night we were on the cruise ship, I told you about my father being killed," he said. "What I didn't tell you is that my mother made our life a living hell. She picked fights with my sister and me. It was constant turmoil in our home. It was like once my father was gone, my mother went off the deep end and created chaos.

"Once I took a knife from my sister. She was determined to kill my mother. I've often wondered if I should've let her. Several times my mother would throw things at us and threaten to harm us. It was just not a good environment for a child."

They walked along in silence.

"It's the reason I've never considered marriage. It's the reason I've only been close to a few women in my life. I'm afraid of getting married. I'm afraid of leaving behind a family with no father figure."

She nodded. "I can understand that. But what are you missing out on because of your fear?"

So much and he was certain that eventually she would kick him to the curb if he didn't ask her to marry him.

She laughed. "I've failed several times at trying to get married. I understand."

"You do?"

"Yes," she said.

"These last few months together," he began, "I've realized that you make me laugh. You drive me crazy, you tease me, you make me feel good about myself, and damn it, I have tried so hard not to fall for you, but I love you, Crystal. I love you more than you will ever know."

Stopping, she pulled him to her and kissed him. The kiss was tender and sweet and he covered her lips with his to take it to the next level. Oh, how he wanted her. He wanted to make love to her. He wanted to wake up beside her each morning. He wanted to grow old beside her, but he was terrified of marriage.

Breaking the kiss, she gazed at him. "I love you, Tyler. With you, I'm happy."

His heart soared with a joy he'd never felt.

Standing on the beach, lit only by the moon, he finally believed. If he didn't ask her to marry him, she would walk away from him forever. She would leave him standing in the sand on the beach and his life would never be the same.

And he had to have her in his life.

Dropping to one knee, he glanced up at her. "I've never asked anyone to marry me before. I don't have a ring. I'm not prepared. Hell, I'm terrified of marriage. I can't live like my mother, sister, and I lived. But with you, when I look in your eyes, all I feel is a warmth that spreads through me and promises me that this is good. That we belong together. That we can create the kind of life we want. And I want that with you. Will you please marry me, Crystal?"

Laughing, she reached down and pulled him up from the sand.

"I love you with all my heart, Tyler. Yes, I'll marry you. And I'm just as terrified as you because this is my fourth engagement. I said I would never do this again, but with you, it feels right. Like you are the missing half of me."

Thrilled, he pulled her into his arms. "I love you, Crystal."

"And I love you," she said. "Whenever you think things are getting too crazy, that I am acting like your sister or your mother, pull me aside and let's talk about it."

"No, I want you to be Crystal, not them," he said.

"And I want to grow old with you, so please be careful. I need you, our children will need you in our lives. But if something should happen to either one of us, we need to promise that we will go on living and taking care of our family."

"Yes," he said. "And try to make certain our children have a normal life."

"Yes," she repeated. "For better or worse."

"In sickness and in health," he said softly, pulling her close and kissing her.

The sound of a baby crying came to them and they broke apart.

"Time to go feed our son," she said.

A feeling of warmth came over him. Baby David would be his son, but he would always tell him about his father.

"Yes," he said. "Time to go take care of him."

They walked hand and hand up to the deck, surprised to see David sitting outside with the baby.

They smiled at him and Tyler reached over and hugged his friend. "She said yes."

David became so excited. "You don't know how happy this makes me. I love both of you and know you're perfect for one another. Now I have one request. Can we have the wedding as soon as possible?"

Crystal picked up the baby and put him to her breast where he happily suckled away.

"My time grows short and I would love nothing more than to see you wed."

They glanced at one another, the fear in their eyes, and yet Tyler knew with certainty that it felt right.

"How soon?"

"Next weekend?"

Again, he glanced at Crystal and she nodded.

"We'll make it happen," he said, his nerves strung tight. He was scared to death but he was about to marry the woman he loved.

"Here on the beach," David said. "Or here on the deck."

"Just a few people," Crystal said softly.

"Agreed," Tyler said.

CHAPTER 27

*C*rystal was planning her fourth wedding and her last. Every day now, there were changes in David and she wanted him to see them married. He had brought them together, even though they met on the cruise first.

It was a happy time and a sad time and she had so many mixed emotions.

She'd found a wedding dress and had it shipped right away. Nothing big or fancy, but just a nice white dress that was long in the back and mid-calf length in the front. They'd found a caterer and a preacher to marry them. The flowers were ordered and she'd asked all three of her friends to stand up beside her.

David was going to be Tyler's best man. They had invited a few close friends and family and she hoped it would be a simple, elegant, and happy affair.

While they had not wanted a reception, David had insisted. So they arranged for a sit-down dinner with a small band where they would dance the evening away.

Maria, who was so excited that she was trusted, was going to take care of Baby David.

After seeing David's coloring and the way he continued to go downhill, they had decided that they didn't need a honeymoon. They wanted to be here with him for as long as they could.

It was hard to think of losing him on this joyous day, but it was an eventuality. They had come to accept it and wanted every waking moment they could have with him before he was gone.

Tyler's mother had been upset that she had not met Crystal and his sister was in agreement, but they were going to attend. Crystal hoped for Tyler's sake that they behaved. And how they would accept Baby David, she didn't know, but her son would not be mistreated by anyone.

"Are you ready?" Jennifer asked. "You know I got married on the beach and it was the best day. Look outside, it's sunshiny and over seventy degrees with a clear sky. I'm so happy for you, Crystal. I think you've found yourself a keeper."

"Thank you, Jennifer," she said. "It feels right."

"Good," Amanda said. "You give me hope."

"And me," Nicole said. "Last time, we warned you not to go through with it, and now we all think this is perfect. And I'm so glad you're doing this before David passes."

"Me too," Crystal said. "That's why we rushed everything. He's been holding on for so long. First to see his son born and now to see Tyler and me get married. After this, I don't know what will keep him fighting."

They all gave her a hug and she wiped her tears away.

"Honey, there comes a point when it's more painful for him to stay. He's fast approaching that point."

"I know, but we love him so much and he's Baby David's father," she said. "I just wish he could be here and be the old strong David."

If only that was possible.

"Are you guys going on a honeymoon?" Nicole asked.

"No, we're not leaving David. We're here until he passes and then we'll have to find a new place to live."

"You're going to miss this gorgeous house," Jennifer said.

"I'm going to miss David even more," she replied.

"Yes, you will," Jennifer admitted.

"I hear music being played. I think that's our cue," Amanda said.

It was time to marry the man who she had hated and then fallen in love with. A man who was just as afraid of marriage as she was. A man who had been nothing but kind to her and given her so much. Who would love Baby David as much as she did. A man she looked forward to creating a future with. She couldn't wait to become his wife.

"Let's go, ladies. I have a man downstairs I want to say *I do* to," she said, picking up her bouquet.

Walking down the stairs, her knees were knocking with fear. What if this wasn't right? What if he didn't love her enough?

Suddenly a stillness overcame her and she was certain. Tyler was the man she loved and they were going to be happy. Very happy.

When she stepped out onto the deck, Tyler was waiting for her with David alongside him in the wheelchair. Her friend beamed at her with a myriad of emotions playing across his face.

Tyler gazed at her and then took her hand. "You look beautiful. I'm so happy I'm marrying you."

"Me too," she said.

About twenty people sat on the deck. The perfect size for a wedding.

Turning to face one another, they said their vows gazing into each other's eyes. This was the flawless wedding for her. None of her previous engagements would've had such a beautiful ceremony here on the beach with the waves crashing.

"You may kiss your bride," the officiant said.

She gazed into Tyler's eyes and knew that she'd made the right decision that day to run away and go on that cruise. The cruise that changed her life forever.

His lips covered hers in a way that promised her so much more. For the last week, they had not shared the same bed. They had never had sex and tonight they would experience the love that had grown between them.

Cheers sounded around them, and when they broke apart, they turned to David.

"Thank you," she said.

"Yes, you brought us together," Tyler told him.

All David could do was nod as tears streamed down his face. "I want you to be happy. I want you to love each other until death parts you and for you to raise my son as your own."

"You know I will," Tyler said, clasping his friend to him.

Maria stood in the doorway holding the baby. She wiped away her tears and turned to the crowd. "Dinner is served downstairs."

The crowd moved to the dining room except for two women. Tyler took her arm and led her to them.

"Mother, I'd like you to meet Crystal," she said.

"Samantha, Crystal," he said to his sister.

"Welcome to the family," she said.

His mother stared at her, and for a moment, Crystal was afraid she was going to be rude, but then she softened.

"I think I knew your mother," she replied. "Did she work at the school?"

"Yes," Crystal responded. "She worked there for fifteen years."

"She died in a car accident, right?"

"Yes," Crystal said. "Her, my father, and my sister."

"She was a lovely woman and I was so sad to hear what happened," she said. "Welcome to the family."

"Thank you," she said relieved. "Please come inside."

After they went in, there were toasts. The first one came from David.

"Sometimes life throws people together for a good cause. Tyler has been my attorney for many years, and Crystal and I met with a goal. I'm dying and I wanted a son and she wanted a baby. Tyler fought us tooth and nail on this, but in the end, I convinced him this was what I wanted, not knowing that in the end, they would marry. To Tyler and Crystal, may you raise my son to be a good man. May your life together be everything I could have hoped for and more."

Everyone raised their glass of champagne and toasted to them, and Crystal's heart swelled with love.

The evening went by quickly, but there was one last thing she had to do before it ended.

SECRETS OF A RUNAWAY BRIDE

"I know our wedding is kind of unconventional, but if you didn't know, we're unconventional people," she said.

"I'll second that," Tyler replied, grinning at her.

"Normally, the bride would throw her bouquet, but I want to give mine to my dear friend."

She walked over and gave Amanda her flowers. "May you find the happiness I've found. You deserve it."

Amanda gasped and then clasped her close. "Thank you, but I'm not certain I'll ever marry again."

"Yes, you will," the three of them said at once and everyone laughed.

David came to them and hugged them. "I have to go to bed. I'm exhausted. I'll see you in the morning."

"Yes," they told him. "Sleep well."

Soon after the guests began to leave and when everyone was gone, she gazed at Tyler and grinned. "Your mother was on her best behavior."

"Yes, I was shocked," he said. "And now that everyone is gone, it's our time."

She grinned at him. "Let me feed the baby, so he'll sleep through the night, and then I'm all yours."

"Really? It seems like we've waited forever."

"I know. And I can hardly wait for you another second."

He grinned. "Come on, let's find our son and get him settled for the night."

CHAPTER 28

*I*t was the first week of December, and Tyler sat beside his friend's bed. In the last week, he and Crystal had taken turns spending the night sitting up beside him. He was not going to die alone.

The hourglass sands were falling faster and faster, and there was nothing anyone could do to stop them.

Most of the time, he slept, but occasionally he would ask about the baby. He and Tyler would talk about old times when they first met each other.

The pain had grown intolerable and he now received doses of morphine to keep him comfortable. They spent most of the day beside his bed, helping him with whatever he needed. Offering comfort when they could. Just being with him.

Crystal walked in with Baby David in her arms and gazed at Tyler. "How is he?"

"Not good," he said. "I don't think it will be long. He's struggling to breathe now."

The hospice nurse was in the living room if they needed

her. All she did was make him comfortable and wait for the end.

David opened his eyes and gazed at them. He saw his son and gave a half smile.

"Can I hold him?"

"Of course," Crystal said, putting the baby in his weak arms. She and Tyler were nearby in case something happened. But David held the infant and gazed down at the child.

"Thank you."

He gave the boy a kiss and then motioned for Crystal to take him.

"I want to go outside," he said. "Roll my bed outside on the deck. I want to see the sunset."

Maria came to the door and she took the baby from Crystal. The housekeeper's eyes filled with tears as she watched Crystal and Tyler unlock and roll his hospital bed through the open glass doors onto the deck.

The sun was slowly sinking, the sky creating a magnificent display of orange and purple. They raised the head of the bed so he could watch the sun go down.

"So beautiful," he said with a sigh.

"Yes," Crystal said and she glanced at Tyler.

They were losing him.

They each took his hand as he closed his eyes.

"We love you," Crystal said as tears rolled down her cheeks.

"Rest in peace, my friend," Tyler said, drops streaming down his face. "Go toward the light."

With a gasp, David's long, painful journey ended. They remained by his side, crying as his heart stopped and he slowly released the grip of their hands.

Death was always painful, but Tyler thought his heart would burst from the excruciating heartache. Even though he'd known for months that his friend was dying, it felt like someone had ripped the bandage off an open wound leaving him gasping at the pain.

David was gone, and Tyler and Crystal held onto one another, knowing that life would never be the same as they cried at the loss of their dear friend who had brought them together.

CHAPTER 29

*T*welve years later.

Crystal watched as David helped his younger brothers and sister fly a kite on the beach. At twelve years of age, the boy looked like a younger version of his father and had a kind heart and soul that she loved so very much.

She glanced at her husband who was watching the kids play.

"How did we get so lucky?"

"David," he said.

After their friend had died, they learned that he had given them the beach house with a written note telling them to fill it will children. And they had.

Besides David, they had four children and finally, Crystal had said enough. She was done having babies.

"He would be so proud of his son," Tyler said. "The boy is so good to the others. We're so lucky he's in our life."

"Yes," Crystal said. She loved all her children, though David had a special place in her heart. "He's growing up so fast."

"And he's taking quite the interest in his father's company."

"All of our children are wonderful," she said, truly believing she was blessed. Finally, the hole in her heart was filled with the family she had longed for.

"This morning he asked me for the birthday video from his dad. I was afraid it would make him sad, but he said that David had a birthday cake and blew the candles out, getting wax all over himself and the cake. He told me his father was a funny man. He said his message this year was about what it meant to be a preteen boy and even told him a funny story about himself. I'm so thankful David made those videos."

For a moment, Tyler was quiet and she knew he was remembering his friend. "He was the best. Our children all have college funds because of him. We have this house and David will graduate college and take over a business. And he brought us together."

"And we were both so afraid of marriage."

"As we should have been," he said. "But it's been the best twelve years of my life. I love you more today than I did when we said I do, and I loved you so very much then. And thank goodness, you're nothing like my mother."

She said, "And to think you didn't want to help me remove that dreadful wedding dress."

He laughed. "Oh no, I wanted to remove it, and then do more to you, which took almost a full year."

"You were a patient man," she said.

"And you were worth the wait," he replied.

"I love you Tyler and the life we have created."

"Me too, and every day I thank David for what we have," he said. "Our home, our life together, and most of all, his son."

They gazed out at their family playing together on the beach and reached for each other's hand. Life was good.

* * *

THANK you for reading Secrets of a Runaway Bride. The idea for this book came to me a year ago and I wanted so badly to write it, but had other commitments. And then when I started it, I was so afraid I was not going to give this story as much creativity as it deserved. This one came from my heart and will linger there for a long time. I hope you enjoyed reading it as much as I enjoyed writing this story. Quickly, Secrets of Mustang Island, is becoming a favorite series of mine. If you haven't read Jennifer's story grab it. The third book Secrets From the Past, will be out in the fall.

PLEASE LEAVE A REVIEW

Did you enjoy the book? Reviews help authors. I would appreciate you posting a review.

Follow Sylvia McDaniel on Facebook.

Sign up for my New Book Alert on my website and receive a complimentary book.

SECRETS OF A SUMMER PLACE

Hollywood, California

Staring at the envelope in her hand, Jennifer Moss sat in her Volvo waiting to pick up her son from the Hollywood high school baseball practice. Before she left the house, she'd grabbed the mail.

Now, an eerie sense of foreboding spiraled through her and filled her with anxiety. But then every time she received a piece of mail in which she didn't recognize the name on the envelope, her stomach churned.

Could this be from her? How many times had she gotten her hopes up for them only to be dashed? Would this be the same?

A soft breeze blew through the window on the cloudless day. For a moment, she stopped breathing as she stared at the address.

Madison Wilson, Austin, Texas.

Who did she know in Austin? Who was Madison Wilson? Anytime she received an envelope like this, her heart would pound in her chest and she would wonder if she'd been discovered.

Part of her wanted to be found, but then she would think of her life now. No one knew. It had been her secret for twenty-six years.

The memory of the house on Mustang Island overwhelmed her. She'd never returned after that summer, and since her parents' deaths, the house sat vacant. As much as she loved that place, she'd never go back because she would have to face the past.

A past that was heart wrenching and left her scared and hating her family.

Shouts from the field alerted her that the team would be leaving practice shortly. The coach always ended their practice with a pep rally. The kids were a good team and might make it to state this year. For her son's sake, she hoped so.

With a sigh, she tore open the envelope and pulled out the letter.

My name is Madison Wilson. According to the genealogy report, your DNA and my DNA are linked. It says you're my birth mother. I would like to speak to you and find out why you gave me up for adoption. I would also like to learn my medical background and even see if we have anything in common. If you are willing to speak to me, please contact me at...

A cry escaped her and the memories flooded her of that terrible day. Her name was Madison. Her heart leaped with a joy only a mother could feel.

Madison gave her address, her phone number, and even her email address.

It had taken twenty-five years, but her secret was about to be revealed. With a sigh, she stared out at the baseball field

SECRETS OF A SUMMER PLACE

and let the memories of that day overwhelm her. How she had clung desperately to her child until her mother ripped the infant from her arms and gave her to the nurse.

She'd never seen the baby again after that day. Tears filled her eyes and trickled down her face. How many times had she thought of finding her and telling her how much she wanted to keep her? In the end, she thought it better not to disrupt her life and had done her best to move on. Now that child was grown up and wondering why she had not been wanted.

But the opposite was true.

Oh, God, how she'd wanted to keep her. To love her and raise her as her own.

That time in her life had been the worst, and she'd never forgiven her mother for forcing her to give up her child for all the right reasons. They were not what Jennifer wanted to hear.

Sometimes doing the right thing was not the easiest. And having that child taken from her arms was gut-wrenching.

Her handsome son walked across the school yard, his head down. Quickly she wiped the tears from her eyes and shoved the letter into her purse.

How was her family going to react to this news?

Her husband Ryan didn't know about her unwed pregnancy and subsequent birth. Her two smart, intelligent, beautiful children had no idea they had a half-sister. This secret had remained hidden for twenty-five years, but no more.

The door opened and her son slid in.

"Hi, Mom," he said and she could see he was upset.

"Bad day?" she asked.

"Kind of," he replied as he looked out the window of the car.

Something had been eating at him and she didn't know what. He refused to talk to her about it, and only said, *I'm okay.* But he wasn't. His grades had gone from honor roll to barely passing and she feared he was going to lose his scholarship to his favorite school.

No matter how she tried to approach him, the walls came slamming down. And today's mail wouldn't make the situation any easier. Yet, she had waited so long for this letter. So long to hear from the baby she loved instantly.

He looked at her and studied her for a moment. "Are you all right?"

"Sure," she said, wondering how he could tell something was up. "Got something in my eye a moment ago."

"Oh," he said and gazed back out the window as she pulled out of the school parking lot.

"Is Dad going to be home tonight?"

"I don't know," she said. "This morning he left early because it's his surgery day."

Alex made a noise she couldn't quite interpret.

Her husband was a leading plastic surgeon in the Hollywood community and had worked on many stars in his practice. The money he brought in had made it easy for her to stay home and raise their two children.

But the hours he worked were sometimes long, and he often came home exhausted. Lately, he seemed to work longer and longer, though he'd promised her he was going to cut back his hours.

In the twenty years they'd been married, she often wondered if she'd traded love for money. Their marriage was good, but they spent so little time together, with him working so many hours. Sometimes it felt like they were two individual people living in the same house.

And there were days she felt lonely. If not for the kids, she would spend her evenings alone. And even they were growing up and moving on with their lives. Taylor would soon finish her second year of college, and next fall, Alex would be going to a university.

"How's the team doing?"

"If we continue to win, we should make the high school playoffs," he said, staring out the window.

Alex was normally so happy and excited and eager to talk, but in the last two months, he'd withdrawn into himself and she couldn't find a way to bring him out. The kid should be so excited about his team making the playoffs, and yet he didn't act like he cared.

Something was eating at her son and she missed the happy-go-lucky young man who was eager to begin his life.

"That's great news," she said. "When's your next game? Maybe me and your dad can both attend."

Ryan had only made it to one game. One, and soon their son's season and high school career would be at an end. Sometimes she hated Ryan's job, even though their life was luxurious because of his career.

That didn't excite Alex and she knew she had to learn what troubled him.

Sometimes she wished Ryan was an accountant or even a salesman and not a busy doctor.

Maybe after Alex graduated, she would get them reservations at Cozumel and take the kids down to the beach. She doubted that Ryan would take the time off. But it would be good to spend some time with her children.

The thought of Madison crossed her mind and she wondered if she would like to go with them.

"That would be nice," he said. "The next game is Saturday morning."

That was Ryan's tee time. Surely he could give up golfing one Saturday for his son. But nothing came between Ryan and his golf.

They pulled into the drive and the gate opened automatically. She pulled into the back garage. The pool man had been here today, and maybe later tonight, she'd get in the water and swim a few laps.

Closing the garage door, they both exited the car and walked into the house, entering through the laundry room.

"Good afternoon, Mrs. Moss, Alex," the maid said to her. "Dinner is in the oven. I'm leaving for the day."

"Thank you, Esmeralda," she said softly.

Alex walked past the woman and that was so unusual for him. Normally he would hug Esmeralda and tell her the cooking was divine. But not today.

Glancing at her son, Jennifer was worried. Maybe it was time to suggest counseling. Anything to keep his grades from falling even further. Anything to keep him from losing his scholarship. Anything to bring the boy she loved back to her.

"Good night," Esmeralda called as she exited the back door.

Jennifer walked into the massive kitchen and there was a salad sitting out and a casserole ready to turn on in the oven.

"Mom," Alex said, walking back into the kitchen. "Coach said I had to give you this."

She glanced at the envelope he held in his hand.

Taking it, she opened it to the letter inside.

"Damn it, Alex," she said as she read the letter. "What is going on?"

He shrugged. "Don't know."

"If you don't bring your grades up you're going to lose your scholarship. You're about to be kicked off the baseball team. This is not my son. Tell me what's wrong."

With a grimace, he turned and walked out of the kitchen. "Maybe I want to do high school over again. Maybe I'm a loser."

"Alex, don't walk away. Let's sit down and talk about this."

He ignored her and went up the stairs to his room.

Shaking her head, she couldn't wait for Ryan to get home. They had to have a serious talk with Alex, and she had to tell him she had another child. Madison.

Reaching inside the refrigerator, she pulled out a full bottle of wine and poured herself a glass.

It was going to be a hell of a night.

Available at Your Favorite Retailer

Contemporary Romance
Burnett Brides Contemporary Times
Travis

Tanner

Tucker

Joshua

Jacob

Justin

Return to Cupid, Texas
Cupid Stupid

Cupid Scores

Cupid's Dance

Cupid Help Me!

Cupid Cures

**Cupid's Heart

Cupid Santa

**Cupid Second Chance

Cupid Charmer

Cupid Crazy

Cupid's Bachelorette

Return to Cupid Box Set Books 1-3

Cupid Help Me Box Set Books 4-6

**The Unlucky Bride

Contemporary Romance
My Sister's Boyfriend

The Wanted Bride

The Reluctant Santa

The Relationship Coach

Secrets, Lies, & Online Dating

Bride, Texas Multi-Author Series
**The Unlucky Bride

Lipstick and Lead 2.0
Nailing the Hit Man
Nailing the Billionaire
Nailing the Single Dad

Secrets of Mustang Island
Secrets of a Summer Place
Secrets of a Runaway Bride
Secrets From the Past

The Langley Legacy
Collin's Challenge

Short Sexy Reads
Racy Reunions Series
Paying For the Past
Her Christmas Lie
Cupid's Revenge

Western Historicals
A Hero's Heart
Second Chance Cowboy
Ethan

American Brides
**Katie: Bride of Virginia

Angel Creek Christmas Brides

Charity

Ginger

Minnie

Cora

The Burnett Brides Series

The Rancher Takes A Bride

The Outlaw Takes A Bride

The Marshal Takes A Bride

The Christmas Bride

Boxed Set

Lipstick and Lead Series

Desperate

Deadly

Dangerous

Daring

**Determined

Deceived

Defiant

Devious

Lipstick and Lead Box Set Books 1-4

**Quinlan's Quest

Mail Order Bride Tales

**A Brother's Betrayal

**Pearl

**Ace's Bride

Scandalous Suffragettes of the West

****Abigail
Bella
Mistletoe Scandal**

Southern Historical Romance
A Scarlet Bride
Charity

The Cuvier Women
Wronged
Betrayed
Beguiled
Boxed Set

** Denotes a sweet book.

**Want to learn about my new releases before anyone else?
Sign up for my New Book Alert and receive a free book.**

USA Today Best-selling author, Sylvia McDaniel obviously has too much time on her hands. With over eighty western historical and contemporary romance novels, she spends most days torturing her characters. Bad boys deserve punishment and even good girls get into trouble. Always looking for the next plot twist, she's known for her sweet, funny, family-oriented romances.

Married to her best friend for over twenty-five years, they recently moved to the state of Colorado where they like to hike, and enjoy the beauty of the forest behind their home with their spoiled dachshunds Zeus and Bailey. (Zeus has his own column in her newsletter.)

Their grown son, still lives in Texas. An avid football watcher, she loves the Broncos and the Cowboys, especially when they're winning.

www.SylviaMcDaniel.com
Sylvia@SylviaMcDaniel.com
The End!

www.ingramcontent.com/pod-product-compliance
Lightning Source LLC
Chambersburg PA
CBHW071552200626
46811CB00028B/2718